SHAMELESS

A TROPICAL AUTHORS NOVEL

STEVEN BECKER   DAVID BERENS   CHRIS NILES

DOUGLASS PRATT

DOWN ISLAND PRESS

INTRODUCTION

Welcome

Tropical Authors has numerous writers who set their books in tropical climes, on islands, under the water, and along the coast.

The four of us came together and created this story to support Tropical Authors.

Shameless is one of several "Less is More" collaborations by our authors. You can check out the rest here.

We hope you enjoy the book and thank you for supporting Tropical Authors.

MAP

Check out the interactive map showing the locations in the book
https://www.google.com/maps/d/u/1/edit?mid=
1m9Bf4baq14gQGkYyqD-NtSg-83qVRmQ&usp=sharing

PART I

DAVID BERENS

David Berens is the USA Today Bestselling Author of the highly-read Troy Bodean Tropical Thriller series, the rip-roaring Ryan Bodean Action Adventure series, and the spine-tingling Chris Collins CIA Thrillers.
To read more by David Berens visit www.BerensBooks.com. Sign up for the BeachBum Brigade newsletter for a few free books while you're there.

PROLOGUE

SHAMELESS
DAVID BERENS

THE MAN with the gun was gone, but I don't know when he left. Time has no meaning here. It's dark all day and all night, and I can't tell when one ends and the next begins.

I'm shivering in the same summer dress I was wearing when they took me. It was beautiful before, pink flowers on a background of yellow, but now it's covered with mud and sweat. If I ever make it out of here, I'm throwing it away.

I don't know how long I've been here, but it's a long time. The room is smaller than the closet in my old house. I can take three steps across the front wall by the metal door. Four steps to the back wall. Fourteen steps around. The first few days I tried to keep moving, to keep counting, but what's the point? I can't get away from the stench of the stuff in the bucket. But at least they gave me a bucket, I guess?

I sit in the corner and stretch out my legs to ease the pain that's started to climb from my knees to my hips from sitting so long on the damp concrete floor. I guess this is why Mom always told me—

My eyes fill with tears at the thought of her. My cheeks are still sticky from all the times I've cried before today, but what else am I going to do? So I cry some more.

Another long time goes by without anyone coming. I wonder if maybe they forgot me, and left me for dead. My stomach flips at the thought of slowly starving to death. I start to panic. It's hard to breathe, and it feels like a bear is sitting on my chest.

A sound. A stream of light bounces through the crack under the door. The man is whistling like he always does, something happy and bright, like he enjoys coming to see the girl in the cage. It makes me sick.

Then, something new. A cross between footsteps and something being dragged. Grunts and yelps—a high voice. Like a kid. Like me.

The door flies open and I scuttle to the back wall like a crab, knocking over the bucket. The man's flashlight shines in my eyes, and I can't see a thing. But a girl cries out. He shoves her with a grunt, and she collapses against me in the puddle of muck from the bucket.

I get a glimpse of her long brown ponytail and red dress before the door slams shut and we're trapped in the darkness again.

The girl doesn't wake up for a long time. I drag her into the back corner as far away from the spill as I can. I check her out as best I can in the dark. Her ankle is swollen and there's a pretty big knot on the back of her head, but I don't feel any cuts. No blood.

She finally stirs, and I sit beside her, holding her hand so she's not scared when she wakes up. I ask her name. I tell her my name, and that I'll watch out for her. Her body shakes a little and then her head drops back down. Passed out. She needs help.

As I wait, my foggy mind begins to clear and I begin to plan. The next time I see the flashlight, I'll be ready.

She stirs three more times before the light comes on again. Each time she stays awake just a little longer, but she doesn't speak. So when the man comes, I shake her awake. Her head lolls and I whisper, "Wake up. I need you. This is our chance." She wobbles a little as she tries to sit up.

I crouch against the wall beside the door and wait.

The light appears.

I hear the man whistle, then the jangling of his keys.

When the door flies open, I pounce.

I throw my body as hard as I can against his legs. They collapse and he falls. His face smashes into the doorframe and he grabs his nose. Blood pours down and he screams in Spanish. The flashlight clatters to the ground, throwing light in a big, bright flood down the hall. I see thick yellowed paint peeling from industrial concrete blocks. There are no windows and no doors, only a long corridor leading into blackness.

I grab the man's light and scream at the girl.

"We have to go. Now!"

I grab her by the wrist and pull her to her feet. She nods, eyes wide, and stumbles after me.

We run as fast as we can down the hall. I hear the man clambering to his feet and shouting. Icy fear fills my heart as I realize we are likely running into the arms of another of our captors.

But I don't care.

I pull the girl along, determined that we will not spend another second in that cage. The floor is rough as if it's made of dirt and rock, and my foot catches on something sharp. I trip but don't fall. I don't slow down. I tug the girl along behind me as I feel a trickle of warm blood on my bare feet.

We round a corner and there's another man. His arm stretches out faster than I can react. He clotheslines me, sending us both flipping backward in a heap. My head hits the ground and for a second, I think I'm going to pass out. The other girl shrieks, terrified.

And, God rest her soul, that is likely what saved my life.

I lay still. Play dead in the shadows by the wall. The man who stopped us leans over the girl. He tells her to SHUT UP SHUT UP SHUT UP. In English, with a thick Spanish accent. But the girl keeps screaming. The man kneels down to clap his hand over her mouth.

Out of the corner of my eye, I see the girl pull her legs up to her chest. She lashes out with strength I didn't think possible. Her heels smash into the man's mouth. He stumbles backward and spits out a bloody tooth. Without saying a word, he draws a pistol from his belt and stands over her as she lies moaning and crying.

The flashlight is still lying on the ground, its beam shining on the wall. Across the room, I see garage doors wide enough to drive a truck through. One of them is open at the bottom, but just a few inches. Is it enough? Can I wiggle through before the man shoots me?

I have to try.

He raises his arm and aims at the girl. His attention will turn to me with his next breath. God forgive me, it's now or never. I roll over on my stomach and scramble across the jagged floor, tearing my arms up in the process, but I don't care. Through the opening, I can see the night sky. Tears stream down my face as I reach the door and roll under it into the cool air. I breathe deep, staring up at the stars.

A gunshot shocks me out of my reverie. And the night goes deadly silent. I flick off the flashlight, rise to my feet, and run.

I run faster than I ever have before, ignoring the pain, fully expecting to be shot in the back at any second. I run through scraggy desert trees, knowing that dogs could be on my trail in moments. I will be caught. Of course, they'll come after me.

But for now, I am free, and I can run.

Just before daylight, I come to a small ranch. I dive into the first shelter I see and cover myself with as much hay as I can. I wait, hens clucking softly above me.

1

SHAMELESS
DAVID BERENS

THIRTEEN YEARS LATER

"Harvey?"

The voice startled me, pulling me out of my restless sleep.

"Martha?" I called out.

And then the realization hit me as it had on so many other occasions—I was dreaming. I could hardly believe I had slept at all. It was cold, colder than it should have been, for chrissakes. So much for escaping the Boston winter. I picked up my watch with an unceremonious groan. Back pain from years of moving couches and beds from one end of the family furniture store to the other—an old retail trick to make it seem like new merchandise had come in—had turned my aching body into that of a frail old man. That and the fact that I was approaching my sixty-eighth birthday made me feel like I was made of ice ready to crack and shatter. I wrapped the heavy watch around my wrist. I hadn't worn a watch since I retired, but Martha, God rest her soul, had bought it for me for our anniversary. The accident took her before she could give it to me—random, senseless, and deadly. Cops couldn't do anything, and it took me a lot of years before I realized there really wasn't much they could do except send me away with a pat on my back.

After the accident, I had found it in her nightstand drawer along with a card telling me that every good sailor needed a dive watch. I had no damned intention of putting my body into the water, but if I ever did, I'd know what time it was with Swiss precision and accuracy. The luminescent pips on its face told me I had woken up long before I should have. Even nearing my seventies, I've always been a good sleeper.

At least I was until my daughter went missing.

Martha and I had never had children. God had deemed both of us unworthy of propagating the human race. No one bearing the Thackerson name would carry on at the furniture store, so Martha came up with the idea that we should adopt. My first reaction was that she was crazy. Two nearly old farts caring for a baby? Not a chance. But she was persistent and suggested that we adopt an older child.

"It's not just about babies, Harvey," she told me. "There are older children in this world who don't have parents. Some are from situations so bleak that they just need a roof over their heads and a safe place to sleep. We have so much, Harvey. It's time we gave some of that back."

And that was the year our daughter came to live with us. Victoria was a beautiful young lady whose family had, well, we didn't know many details, but it was a horror. When she came to us, she was skin and bones, probably abused, but she had beautiful dark hair and eyes. Martha wrapped her love around the girl and showered her with peace and security. Some children are not born to you. Some children are serendipitous gifts from God. Our daughter came straight from heaven ... or at least, that was what I had thought.

To keep her close to home after she graduated from high school, we chose to send Victoria to Bunker Hill Community College. She was reluctant, hoping to break free and spread her wings a bit, but we agreed if she made it through a couple of years, we'd talk about an apartment or dorm at a four-year college.

As it turned out, she flourished at Bunker Hill, actually staying on there for almost three years. She enrolled in their Global Languages concentration, and being fluent already in Spanish and English, she thrived. She got a job working on campus at the DISH Food Pantry and even played for the soccer team. Go Bulldogs! Martha and I went to all her games, and on more than one occasion explained that, no, we were not Victoria's grandparents. By the time she finished her career at Bunker Hill, she had become the team's leading scorer and had served hundreds of people at the pantry. I'm not sure Martha and I could have been prouder.

Upon receiving her associate's degree—graduating as a Commonwealth Honors Scholar— she decided to stay nearby and attend Boston College. I still remember the day she laid her acceptance letter on the kitchen table and craftily slid an apartment rental agreement alongside it.

"You said we would talk about it," she said. "This one is close to the college, so I won't even need a car. I can walk back and forth to class and the grocery store. It's perfect."

I was reluctant, but Martha insisted that it was time to let our girl stretch her wings and fly a little.

"Every little bird must leave the nest sometime," she told me while filling out the application.

The next couple of years were typical college years. Victoria chose to double major in linguistics and perspectives of Spanish America. I proudly told all of the Tuesday-night poker guys that she would soon be the most educated Thackerson who had ever lived. They duly clapped me on the shoulder and raised their glasses of whiskey to toast Victoria's future.

She probably could have played for BC's soccer team, but with a double major, she decided it wasn't worth pursuing. She did, however, continue her path of service by working at a local after-school program. She really had a way with people, especially kids.

And before I could blink an eye—time has a way of rushing past you when you're older—she had amassed the hours needed to graduate. She had completed her double major, kept her spotless grade-point average, and had been presented with the Wendy Berson

Language Award, as well as the Boston College General Excellence Award. Our home phone had begun ringing off the hook with calls from international companies looking for someone like Victoria. The world was her oyster.

I bought a new tie, Martha picked out a new dress, and we planned a little party for our girl. Martha reminded me how we had opened our home to this beautiful, smart, ambitious girl who never would have had the opportunities open to her now if we hadn't taken a chance on adoption. As I practiced tying my new tie, I realized just how proud I was of Victoria. I didn't even have to tell the poker guys ... they knew it from the look on my face. Everything was sailing along—until it came time for her diploma ceremony.

2

SHAMELESS
DAVID BERENS

ONE AFTERNOON, Victoria came into the living room in tears. Being so close by, she often stopped over for dinner and laundry day. Sometimes she was down about a tough test or assignment at school but this was different. She slumped down on the couch and held out a crumpled piece of paper.

"It was stuffed in my mailbox at the apartment," Victoria said, wiping her face. "I can't believe it. This has never happened before."

Martha wrapped her arms around her while I read the letter.

"If you show up to the graduation ceremony, there will be serious consequences," the note read. "We don't want your kind here."

The handwriting was shaky and the spelling was atrocious: *graduashun* and *consaqwences*. I wanted to tear up the ignorant filth, but Martha insisted we turn it over to the authorities. The letter was promptly whisked off to a government organization with a three-letter name, and we never heard about it again. The Boston P.D. assured us we could go to the ceremony, as there would be officers on hand. Four of Boston's finest to protect two thousand kids. It didn't seem like enough police presence to me, but they assured us it would be fine.

Fearing for our safety and Victoria's, Martha made up some excuse why we couldn't go. Victoria was heartbroken. She'd made so many friends and this sudden, ugly bigotry was a surprise to us all.

She changed after that. She said she was through with Boston and didn't belong here. That single piece of paper had wrecked her self-confidence and the submissive, scared, distrustful girl whom we'd thought we had saved from a life of abuse and hardship had come back. Martha once found Victoria's diary and was not shocked to read that she was planning a serious move. She had a list of places to go, apartments for rent, and classified listings for low-paying, crap jobs.

"I want to go someplace where it NEVER SNOWS!" the last entry read in heavy, dark scribbles.

"This has to stop, Harvey," Martha said. "We can't let this happen. We're not spending enough time with her."

I protested. The store needed me. Victoria made it clear she had no interest in running the family business and, God knows, none of my staff had it in them to take over.

"Sell it, Harvey. It's time to move on," Martha had said. "You and me, we're too old to keep selling settees and ottomans. Let's buy a boat and get out of Boston. It's too cold here for old people like us. Let's take Victoria away from here and go on an adventure. You know, someplace where it never snows."

"I suppose you're gonna tell me you want to go to Florida, too," I joked. But she winked at me and pulled out a pile of brochures. Apparently, she had been making plans of her own to leave town. I promptly trashed all the ones promising shuffleboard, pickleball, bingo nights, and Pilates. I wasn't ready to move into a glorified nursing home and wait to die.

One cheaply made flier caught my eye, though. Shark Key Campground and Marina in Florida. Far enough south to be tropical and warm, and just far enough out of Key West to have a little more of an "old Keys" vibe. Close to a grocery store, but far enough away to have the more laid-back lifestyle we were looking for after retirement. Quiet, serene, laid-back, and no shuffleboard. It was settled.

We packed our things and readied the boat, which Martha had insisted we name *Serendipity*. She had so much fun planning our stops along the coast. She hadn't looked so alive in twenty years. I began to enjoy the thought of it as well. Maybe I had sea legs after all.

3

SHAMELESS
DAVID BERENS

SO THAT FALL, after christening our new boat on a Friday the thirteenth, we had everything packed to make our first grand trip to Florida. Martha was killed the next Friday. The man in the SUV who hit her fled the scene, leaving my angel to die in a matter of minutes. They never found him, though I wasn't sure they tried very hard. Probably a drunk driver, the officers had told me.

In hindsight, I'm not sure I realized just how much the letter had affected Victoria. I also realized that we hadn't been as close to Victoria after she moved out. It's natural for college kids to want some freedom, but she was obviously a special case, with her background and everything that had happened to her.

I realized that all summer through our old-folk boat dreaming and trip planning, we hadn't bothered to include Victoria. Of course, we planned to take her with us, but now I saw that she felt more isolated and overlooked than ever. She left the day after Martha's funeral, taking off while I was attending a grief-counseling meeting down at St. Mary's. No note, no goodbye, no nothing. Not much was out of place in her room. She didn't take anything except a backpack and a few of her things. She left her cell phone on the kitchen counter. I came home from that meeting feeling the tiniest bit better about my life only to find it turned upside down again.

I sat on the living room floor and didn't move for days. I slept on the floor. I talked to God, demanding to know why He would do this to me. And when I finally got up on the third day of my misery, my old bones telling me they couldn't take it anymore, I figured out where Victoria had gone.

I finally took out the heaping trash can and saw the brochures I had thrown away. The happy people playing bingo on the cover enraged me. I ripped up the papers and flung them into the icy wind like confetti. Back inside, I rifled through the junk drawer in the kitchen, determined to get rid of the last evidence of our planned adventure on the boat. But the pamphlet I was looking for wasn't there. The one-page, three-color flier proclaiming that Shark Key Marina and Campground was like paradise, only quieter, was gone.

I grabbed the suitcase I'd packed for our doomed adventure, walked out, and slammed the door behind me. I didn't even bother to lock it. There was a good chance I wasn't coming back.

A few minutes later, I boarded *Serendipity* and readied her for the one-way trip.

4

SHAMELESS
DAVID BERENS

AND HERE I WAS, floating in the dark at Shark Key Campground and Marina. Shark Key is a small island, so it had not taken me long to figure out that Victoria wasn't here. In fact, if the guy at the marina was to be believed, she had never stopped here at all. So I lay awake, drifting in the dark, literally and mentally. I had been so certain I would find Victoria here that I had no backup plan. There was no Plan B. I wondered if she had gotten lost. I wondered if she was huddled on a park bench somewhere between Boston and Florida, or maybe living in a cardboard box. I cursed myself for not driving down instead. I knew it was an impossibility, but maybe I could have found her along the way.

Jesus, what if she'd been kidnapped, taken, shoved into a van ... I immediately put the horrible thoughts out of my mind.

Bolstered by the image of my Victoria living out a repeat of the same horror as before we adopted her, I pulled myself out of bed. I wasn't sure where I was going, but I'd had enough of sitting still while our baby girl was out there alone.

Serendipity was a great old boat, with more emphasis on the *old* than the *great*. I turned the key and she sputtered and cranked, but the engine wouldn't comply. I tried a few more times to no avail. I slammed my hand on the wheel so hard I thought I might have cracked a bone. I had expected this. The long and arduous journey from Boston had put the old girl—and me—through quite a strain. I gave up and went below to put some ice on my hand and prayed I hadn't broken anything. The galley freezer contained a bag of peas, a splash of bourbon, and a pair of freezer-burned enchiladas. I hadn't eaten them because they gave me gas something awful the last time I ate some.

I mentally slapped my palm to my forehead. Gas. I climbed back up and checked the gauge. Sure enough, I was out of gas. Martha would have told me to be thankful. The silver lining was that filling the fuel tanks was an easy fix. Or at least it would be when the normal people of the world woke up this morning.

I decided on the only course of action that really made any sense. I poured the bourbon into a small cup and headed back to bed. I knew I wouldn't sleep. Images of Victoria crying and in pain filled my mind. And of course, I thought of Martha. Not in a million years had I ever thought I would have to live without her. I always just assumed I would go first. She was strong, she would be handling this much better than me.

I choked back the rest of the bourbon and waited. I finally fell into what some folks call a fitful sleep.

It wasn't long before I woke to the sounds of a few fishermen coming out to lay claim to their personal spots—as if anyone could rightfully call any one fishing hole around the island their own. It was still dark, but the horizon was a lighter shade of gray, with some pink around the edges. It was hazy, but in the islands, all you had to do was wait ten minutes and you'd get the weather you wanted.

I ran my hand through what surely looked like Einstein's hair on my head and made my way back into the galley. The can of Folger's was empty and I cursed the fact that I was going to have to make it through the morning without my caffeine fix. Through my daze, I was jolted by the sudden ring from my cell phone. It hadn't rung in days. I glanced at the number before answering. "Protected." That was an odd way to put it. I had seen "Unknown" and "Possible Scam" before, but not "Protected" ... or maybe I had. An old memory tickled the back of my brain.

I tapped the screen and said, "Hello?"

The woman on the other end of the line asked me if I was Harvey Thackerson. I verified my date of birth and my paternal grandfather's middle name.

"Hold, please," she said, and before I could ask who the hell she was, the line crackled and switched over to a Muzak version of "Strangers in the Night."

Boy, that was a loaded song. Martha and I had enjoyed many slow dances to it—the Sinatra version, of course. I was humming to myself when a gruff voice interrupted me.

"Mr. Thackerson?" he asked, sounding for all the world like a drill sergeant.

"Since I was born," I said. "Who is this? What's this all about?"

"Mr. Thackerson, my name is Wayne Cunningham. I work for the U.S. Marshals Service."

My blood became ice. I hadn't heard from them in years. Not since Victoria came into our lives. Apparently, he was still speaking, but I hadn't heard him in my shock.

"Are you still there, Mr. Thackerson?"

"I ... I am," I said weakly.

"As I said, we have recently been handed over a document you provided to the FBI in conjunction with the harassment of one Victoria Vasquez, who we placed with you in the year—"

Hearing him say her former last name, Vasquez, out loud sent a wave of shock through me. Suddenly, I was filled with terror about my missing girl. I had the worst feeling that I knew what had happened to her.

An awkward silence filled the line. I looked down at my phone. I had lost him, the signal dodgy at best in the cabin. I wandered up onto the deck for some fresh air. The memories came flooding back. Martha and I had put in for a normal adoption, but the U.S. Marshals Service had offered us something entirely different. Victoria had escaped from a highly torturous environment with a cartel somewhere south of the border—they wouldn't tell us much. Somehow she'd made it across the border, and in a situation with details that were not disclosed to us at that time, she had entered the witness protection program.

No one had thought it even remotely possible that the cartel—Victoria had told Martha and I a scant few details about it—would find her. I mean, we lived in the middle of Boston, for chrissakes.

My phone rang again.

"Mr. Thackerson?" Cunningham said.

"Yes, yes, I'm still here." I shook the memories away, but the terror stayed behind.

"Well, as I said, we finally got a hit on the letter. It is not conclusive, but the FBI found a match."

"A match?"

"To the handwriting on the letter," he said, paper rustling in the background. "Apparently, it belongs to a man recently arrested trying to sneak into Mexico. Says here he was a thug working for the—"

"Sandoval Cartel," I said, finishing his sentence.

5

SHAMELESS
DAVID BERENS

FOR A LONG MOMENT, the line was silent. It was my turn to ask if he was still there.

"Mr. Thackerson, I am going to pretend that you did not say that," he said, his voice lowering to nearly a whisper. "That information is confidential and should not have been revealed to you unless an emergency situation called for it."

"I suppose that means we have an emergency now, then," I said. "Since you were about to reveal it to me."

He sighed. "We do. The man told us a few things we already knew, but after hearing his choice between a place to stay at Guantanamo or another more ... accommodating location, he told us a few things we did not already know."

"And what does this have to do with Victoria?"

"I am calling to be sure that she is with you, Mr. Thackerson," he said. "We may need to take her in and, I'm sorry to say, she may need to be placed in a new location."

"That is not happening," I said. "You cannot just take my daughter away—"

"Mr. Thackerson," he interrupted me this time. "This is a life or death situation. She is in grave danger, and apparently, her identity was compromised. If you care about Victoria, you need to bring her in and allow us to do our job."

I can't say exactly why I felt this way, but Wayne Cunningham was not telling me everything. He knew something I didn't, and it was going to stay that way. The ice that had been running in my veins was now boiling. Without thinking, I hurled my phone as far as I could into the dark water. It splashed and promptly sank to the bottom. The sunrise was glistening purple and orange on the horizon. The water sloshed gently around the pilings, and somewhere over toward O'Hara Key, an osprey woke up, its high-pitched whistle reminding me of a kettle that was currently not making any coffee.

I shrugged off the cool wind drifting over the boats, my mind a hurricane of thoughts. A smart man would not have thrown his phone into the water. A smart man would have told the U.S. Marshals what had happened and trusted that they could help him find Victoria before the cartel thugs did.

The smell of coffee wafted past my nose and I wondered if I was hallucinating. I glanced up at the marina's office and saw someone moving around inside. The man, who might have been wearing a cowboy hat, definitely had a coffee pot in his hand. Not knowing what to do next, I figured I'd get a cup and warm up.

As I got closer to the door, the man in the hat waved through the glass as he flipped the sign to read Open for Business, and as promised by the sign, opened the door.

"Howdy," he said, his accent pure Louisiana.

"I'll take a *lahge regulah*," I said.

He blinked at me, holding out his hand, and I realized I had slipped back into my native accent, a thick Boston-ese. Completely foreign and undecipherable to anyone south of, well, south of Boston.

"Sorry, son." I took his hand and shook it. "Coffee. I'll take the biggest coffee you have."

"Oh, that," he said, recognition flashing across his eyes. "I hope you like it strong and black, 'cause that's all we got."

"That'll do just fine." I walked to a small counter, and with the slightest stumble, perched myself onto a stool that had the name Kirk

Jockell painted on the top. "Mr. Jockell won't mind if I borrow his chair, will he?"

The man, seeing me stumble, had hooked his hand under my elbow. Even though he was a wiry fellow with only a slight paunch where he likely kept his beer, he was stronger than he looked. He helped ease me onto the stool. "Haven't seen him in a bit. He's probably up in Port St. Joe this time of year."

He slid a large cup of coffee across the counter. I reached toward my back pocket to pay for it, but he held up his hand.

"This one's on me, partner," he said. "Honest, you look like you could use it. Mind if I ask if everything's okay?"

I opened my mouth to say that everything was just peachy, as you do with strangers, but then I stopped. There was something different about this guy. I mean, he looked like everyone else you meet in the Keys—at least on the water. He had long, dark hair that may not have been washed this month, a deep, ruddy tan, cheapo flip-flops, blue-lensed sunglasses hanging around his neck, a neon pink T-shirt with the sleeves cut off proclaiming "Woody's has the coldest beer and the hottest girls," and he topped it all off with a straw cowboy hat.

"What's your name, son?" I asked him.

He extended his hand and shook mine firmly. "Bodean, sir. Troy Clint Bodean."

6

SHAMELESS
DAVID BERENS

"Pleased to meet you, Mr. Bodean," I said, taking a deep breath as I thought about what I was going to say.

"Nah, it's Troy. My dad was Mr. Bodean and I reckon I'd rather not bring him up in this conversation." He laughed as he said it. "And I can see something is bothering you that ain't none of my business. But if there's anything I can do to help out, that's my job here."

I don't know why, but this guy, Troy, made me feel a little calmer about the shitstorm that had befallen my life in the last two months. "Actually, I need to fill up my boat."

"Roger that," he said, wiping the counter with a rag that looked dirtier than the counter.

"Headin' out on the water today?"

"I ... well ... actually ..." I realized I had no idea what I was going to do, or where I might go. My whole plan had been to find Victoria here on Shark Key. But she wasn't here. And if the man on the phone —what was his name?—Wayne Cunningham was right, some bad people were after her.

"I need to find my daughter," I finally said, struggling not to break down in a puddle of emotion in front of this guy. "After my wife died, my girl, my Victoria, she ... she ran away."

"Oh, I get ya," he said and stopped cleaning the bar. "Listen, ain't my concern, but I do know where a lot of people who are runnin' tend to go around here."

"Yeah?"

He nodded. "It's widely known and accepted that everyone who goes to Key West is runnin' from something."

This fellow named Troy spoke with a Southern accent, but from the way he talked and how he said it, I could tell he wasn't stupid. And watching how he was casual, yet precise, it came to me.

"You're ex-military, aren't you, son?" I asked him.

A shadow fell across his face and suddenly his eyes closed off. He didn't shut them, they just turned off as if I'd flicked a switch. I put up my hand.

"Hey, I'm sorry," I said. "I didn't mean to touch that sore spot. I know how it is, Troy. I turned eighteen just as we were pulling out of 'Nam. I joined up. It was complicated back then, but I had my reasons. Thank God, I never saw any combat, but it was still hell. And I'd do it all over again to get my baby out of—"

My throat locked up and I couldn't keep the tears from falling down my cheeks. I looked up, and Troy Bodean was back. His eyes were kind and concerned.

"So, your daughter, Victoria, she's got herself into some trouble?"

I explained why I thought she had come to Shark Key and the whole story of my trip down. In telling it to him, I realized why I had sailed down here. Maybe I was running, too. And maybe, I wasn't planning on going back.

A few quiet moments passed before either of us said anything. A fisherman came in, bought some bait, a six-pack of beer, and some beef jerky. He came and went without much communication except a tip of Troy's hat.

"Harvey," he finally said in a low voice. "I can't do much to help you, but if I was you, and if you think she came this far, I'd check Key West. I'll get you filled up and you can get on your way."

"Much obliged, son," I said, drinking the last of the coffee. "I'll head down and get her ready."

"I'll be down directly," he said, putting on his sunglasses.

7

SHAMELESS
DAVID BERENS

THE MARINA WAS a little more active now. The tourists had come out to play. Families down from the mainland for the weekend were loading up brightly colored floats, water skis, coolers of juice and beer, and the occasional grandparent with those virtual reality goggles covering their reading glasses. The water was rolling from the idiots who did not understand or who refused to follow the no-wake guidelines. *Serendipity*, the thirty-four-foot O'Day cutter Martha had found for us on FloridaSailboatsForSail.com was rocking around, bumping into the dock. The fenders needed replacing. I thought I'd ask Troy if they had any that would work in stock. The old girl was in rough shape, and I don't know how much bumping she could take. True to his word, Troy was down a few minutes later and gassed her up.

"She's a beauty," he said.

I glanced up at the bow. My eyes trailed back along the low-slung cabin windows. She really was a pretty boat, graceful yet simple. A strong wave rippled under us, and even though I've got good sea legs, it threw me off balance. I fell to the deck, elbow first. A loud crack and a shooting pain knifed up my arm. I knew immediately something was wrong, bad wrong, but it didn't feel like a break. I was pretty sure I ran through every curse word I knew and even made up a few. Troy was down beside me in an instant.

"I heard it, too," he said, looking into my eyes. "Take a minute, catch your breath. My truck battery's dead, but I'll go see if I can get someone to jump it and we'll get you to the hospital."

"No, no," I said. "I don't think it's broken. Maybe dislocated or something, but I'm not going to die. I'd rather put a bag of frozen peas on it and get on my way."

"Mr. Thackerson, I'm not sure you can sail in this condition," Troy said. "If you're banged up bad and hit some trouble ..."

He trailed off, leaving me to consider the horrible things that could happen to a one-armed retiree trying to sail a boat.

"Help me up, Troy," I said, cradling my arm. "There's a bag of peas in the freezer down below. Grab it for me, would ya?"

He nodded and helped me to a sitting position. I took a few deep breaths. He disappeared below to get my makeshift ice pack. As I sat trying to calm myself, I looked around the deck of *Serendipity*, taking it all in.

"She's a great boat, you know? She's been my home for a month now," I called to Troy. "It was Martha's dream, really."

I could hear him rummaging around and wondered if I had imagined the peas. Maybe my mind was slipping. I looked down at my arm. "Two tours in the Navy. College hockey. Rebuilding a house in Boston. A month on the water. And then I fall on the deck while sitting at the dock." I groaned. "I really am getting too old for this. You know what I mean, Troy?"

I definitely said this loud enough for him to hear, but he said nothing. A tingling started to slide up my spine. The hair on the back of my neck stood straight up. After everything I'd been through, I knew when to trust my intuition. Something was wrong.

"Troy?" I called out again. Nothing.

8

SHAMELESS
DAVID BERENS

I EASED MYSELF UP, protected my arm, and made my way to the ladder. I somehow climbed down below and was greeted by Troy, standing in the middle of the galley ... with his hands raised in surrender. He widened his eyes slightly, one soldier to another, alerting me to the danger. That was when I saw the man standing behind him with a gun in his back. He had dark hair, dark eyes, and the same Latino complexion as Victoria.

When he saw me, the man started spouting in Spanish. I knew about as much of the language as any nearly seventy-year-old native of Boston knew—which was *very little*—but given his tone, I didn't need to know much. I wondered if U.S. Marshal Wayne Cunningham knew there were thugs on my boat, in the middle of nowhere down in the Florida Keys. How could he? Then again, how in the hell did this guy find me here? As if he read my mind, he held up Victoria's cell phone. I had brought it with me, and I suppose modern cartels were sophisticated enough to track them.

He shouted something else and jabbed Troy in the back with his gun. I caught a glimpse of a silencer. These guys were pros.

"I believe this dude is looking for your daughter," Troy said. And then he did something I'll never forget. He smiled and winked at me.

I was startled, but then I noticed he was flicking his eyes toward the floor. As if I could hear his thoughts, two words jumped into my head: Get down! Just for an instant, I forgot who I was—old man Harvey from Boston. Not a nanosecond passed. I dropped. I fell to the floor, again banging my arm in the process. I nearly fainted from the pain.

In a blur of motion I wouldn't have thought possible from this laid-back, island cowboy, he reached out and grabbed the one-egg pan on the stove, whirled around, grabbed the guy's wrist, and pushed it out of the way. In the same motion, the gun fired, the woofing sound of the silencer still loud in the small space, and Troy slammed the pan into the side of the man's head. The guy's eyes went skyward and he slumped to the ground. As he fell, Troy took his gun and turned it on thug number two, who I hadn't seen behind him. Without hesitation, Troy fired twice. Once in the man's chest and once right between his eyes. Troy bent down and checked the first guy's pulse. Satisfied they were both dead, he turned toward me.

"You okay, Mr. Thackerson?"

"I'm fine. Hurts like the devil, but I'll be fine," I said. "Hand me the cell. We need to get the big guns in on this."

Troy leaned back and picked up Victoria's phone. I clicked it to call Wayne back, but then I realized he'd called me on my cell—the one that was now at the bottom of the Gulf. Even as I considered it, I wasn't sure I could do a callback on a private number, anyway.

"Don't got the number, eh?"

"I think I can get it," I said, pulling myself up with his help.

"Get the police on the line, we'll figure that stuff out later," Troy said.

I tapped the screen, but then turned it off. "But if those two guys were tracking us, could it be that this cell is compromised?"

Troy thought about this for a second. "Could be. Let me run up and call from the shop. You stay here."

"Help me get topside." I grabbed the peas I had been looking for earlier and wished I hadn't emptied the bourbon. "And if there's anything to drink in the shop that'll dull this pain, let me know."

He nodded and stepped onto the dock. He was about to head up to the shop when a voice echoed from the other side, behind the gas pumps. Three women drifted alongside the dock riding rented jet skis, practically licking their lips at the sight of Troy.

"Hey, hey, sexy man. Why don't you bring that beautiful tan of yours over here and"—the most well-proportioned of the ladies paused and winked at her friends—"fill us up?"

Troy looked over at me and I shrugged. *Just fill 'em up and let's get going,* I thought.

They all stepped onto the dock while Troy pumped the gas. And while I say women, I'm pretty sure these were actually men dressed in drag—a redhead, a blonde, and a dark-haired Cher lookalike. Cher was the one who had asked Troy for the gas.

"Ladies." Troy tipped his hat and began to fill the tank of the first jet ski. He motioned toward the marina store. "We've got snacks, drinks, and such up at the shop if you need anything."

"Sugar," said the red-headed drag queen, still wearing a good amount of makeup, though her hair looked like she might have fallen in the ocean once or twice, "the only thing I want to eat up right now is you."

They all cackled in unison and Troy flashed a good-natured smile. "I would love to hang out with you ladies, but there's work to be done."

"All work and no play," Cher said. "Am I right, girls? But I know that story. We've only got another hour or so ourselves, then it's off to work for this bevy of beauties as well."

"Oh, hunny," the girl in the back spoke up in a husky voice ... Marilyn? "Why don't you tell our new friend and his dad over there about the thing."

I arched an eyebrow. I suppose I was old enough to be Troy's father. Troy shrugged and began to fill the second jet ski.

Cher walked toward me with an eyebrow arched higher than I would've previously thought possible. She said nothing but reached into a pocket that shouldn't exist in the tiny bikini she was wearing and pulled out a neon yellow flier. I didn't look at it as it dropped to the dock.

"Dreamgirls Amateur Night," Marilyn said through pouty lips. "Maybe if your son there will show us what he's got, we'll show him the money."

"Mmmhmm," Cher added. "Tonight is a big one, baby. Five-hundred-dollar prize for the best ... shall we say ... beginner."

"Ladies," I said. "I am impressed and flattered that you think my son is appropriate for the contest, but we have serious business to attend to."

Cher gave me a pouty look and scolded me. "Tsk, tsk. Your loss, daddy-o."

"Would you shave that beard, sweetie?" I overheard the third girl say—I couldn't figure out who she was supposed to be, but she had fiery red hair and big green eyes.

"I'd prefer not," Troy said, scratching his chin. The gas pump dinged, indicating the last tank was full.

"All the better, baby," Cher said, winking at him. "We're the judges, and from what I've seen in that bone structure, you could walk away with five big bills tonight."

She waited, again timing her joke, and then looked back at the others and added, "Or maybe even three medium Jills, if you play your cards right."

"We'll see," he said, as they started up the jet skis and pulled away from the dock.

"I gotchu, babe," Cher said, blowing him a kiss.

"See you later, big boy," Marilyn said with a wink.

The redhead just bit her lip and made a "call me" gesture with her hand.

Troy pushed them away from the dock and turned back toward me.

"Sorry about that, Harvey," he said. "I'll go call the cops."

He turned away, leaving me alone, with the gentle wake of the jet skis disappearing in the distance. I glanced down at the flier and froze. There on the front, in black and neon yellow, was a picture of the current Dreamgirls lineup. And second from the left ... was Victoria.

SHAMELESS

DAVID BERENS

"TROY!" I yelled. "Wait."

Under each picture, it had their "name." Cher, Marilyn, Rita—ah, that was the redhead, Rita Hayworth—and several other famous beauties from the ages. And under my Victoria's picture, it said, "Shame." I had no idea what that meant, nor did I care. I knew where to find my daughter.

He walked back to the boat, a look of confusion on his face.

"Troy, she's there. That's her," I said, pointing to the flier. "Get me to Key West, help me get my daughter. I can't do it on my own, and I saw the way you handled those thugs."

He shook his head. "Sir, as much as I'd like to help, I owe rent on my camping spot and I need a new battery for my truck. If I took off now, I'd lose this job and my home."

I thought about it for a second and made a snap decision. "Help me and I'll give you *Serendipity*. Get me to Key West, and when we get there, we'll part ways and the boat is yours. She's been a good home for me, but she deserves better than this old fella can give her."

He laughed until he saw I was serious. "No. No. That's just ... I mean, I can't ... sir, that is really kind of you, but I couldn't do that."

I lifted my arm, new needles of pain shooting through the bruised and swelling limb. "I can't do this on my own. I need your help. Troy, I don't know if you ever had kids, but this is my daughter. She wasn't mine by blood, but she was my baby girl."

He sucked air in over his teeth. "Let's get the truck going. I can get somebody to jump it and—"

"Troy. No," I said, my Boston accent suddenly making my voice sound like JFK—at least to my ears. "I'm not waitin'. You can come with me or not, but either way, I'm heading to Key West right now."

He took a deep breath. He looked back up at the marina. I imagined he might be saying his goodbyes. Troy turned back to me and held out his hand. I wasn't sure what he was asking, and he must've seen the confusion on my face.

"The cell phone, Mr. Thackerson," he said. "We can't take it with us."

I nodded and pulled it out of my pocket. I scrolled through some of the selfies of Victoria on the phone. To his credit, Troy waited patiently ... until I was ready. I handed it to him. Suddenly, he smashed it down on the deck. He picked up the shattered bits of it, pulled the battery out, and threw it as far as he could into the water. It plunked once and then all was silent again.

"Don't really approve of dumping anything like that in the water, but this might be a bit different," he said, mostly to himself.

He wiped his hands together as if washing them of the whole episode.

"Okay, Mr. Thackerson," he said. "I'll borrow Chuck's Wagoneer. I'm in for at least getting you over to Key West. After that, we'll see what's waiting for us. Then I'll get back up here and maybe, with a little luck and sweet talkin', all will be okay."

"And then *Serendipity* is yours," I said.

"Sir, I appreciate what you're tryin' to do," he said, "but that just ain't right to take a man's boat."

"Then I'll sell it to you for five hundred dollars when you win the Amateur Night contest."

I knew I had him with that one. He smiled and shook his head.

"Well, seein' as how I ain't entering the contest, that ain't gonna happen, either."

"Then, we have a deal," I said, holding out my hand.

He took it and shook it, believing that we had made a pact that would never come to fruition. In a few minutes, we were in the "borrowed" Jeep on our way west.

"Young fella," I said, over the sound of the rumbling Wagoneer. "I just realized there are two dead guys on the boat."

"Not your concern, Mr. Thackerson," he said, touching the side of his nose.

I had no idea what that meant, but in the short time I'd spent with him, I had come to trust Troy Bodean.

SHAMELESS
DAVID BERENS

THE WEATHER COULD NOT HAVE BEEN any better. I rolled down my window with some effort—it is incredibly hard to work a manual crank with a bum arm—and for a short time, I was able to push the immediate feeling of dread aside. The pain in my elbow had eased to a dull throb. It was swollen, but not black and blue. The frozen peas had become mush, so I opened the bag and dumped them along the highway. Looking out at the immense ocean to either side of the bridge, sunlight glittering off the waves, I knew Martha would have been in heaven.

When we slowed in tourist traffic, I asked, "Troy, what will you do with those dead thugs?"

"Mr. Thackerson," he said, "it may be best that you don't know about that. Some things are better left unsaid."

I massaged my forearm, where the faded blue tattoos told a story from a long, long time ago. "Troy, I'm a big boy. I don't think anything you tell me now is gonna make one hill of beans of a difference in the long run."

He inhaled through his nose, tipped his straw cowboy hat back, and sucked his teeth. I could tell he was thinking about a solution to our "problem."

"Probably grab some odds and ends from the boat for ballast, wrap it all up in a tarp," he said. "Get 'em out in deep water and chuck 'em overboard. It's likely they'll float up in a few days, but I'm guessing putrefaction and scavengers will leave nothin' but the bones. They'll sink to the bottom and that's a heck of a long way down from here."

"Nothin' that will get us in trouble, right?"

"By the time anyone finds them two fellers—if they ever find 'em —it's not likely to be your problem anymore, sir." He tilted his head in such a way that I got his drift.

I maybe had enough time left on this earth to do one more good thing—rescue my daughter.

"I ain't that old, Troy. I'm not dead yet. I might be ready to retire here in Florida now, but I've got plenty of time to do one more good thing. I will rescue my daughter from the evil that is coming after her," I said in thick Boston-ese. "And who knows? Maybe the boys at Wrigley will win another one before I kick the bucket."

"They might find those dudes first," he said with a grin.

"Shut it, Bodean," I said.

I could picture the scene playing out on the *Serendipity*. I watched in my mind's eye as Troy, without ceremony or worry, dropped the bodies into the water. I imagined a few bubbles erupting from under my old green tarp, sinking slowly into the deep. And I was happy about it.

"Mr. Thackerson," Troy said, bringing me back from my reverie. "You doin' okay?

We were still sitting in slow traffic, but I could see Key West up ahead. One more bridge from Stock Island onto Cayo Hueso.

"Well, in for a penny, in for a pound, eh, Troy?" I said. "Guess we're wanted men now, what with those dead guys and all. Wonder which three-letter organization will be after us."

"Naw," he said, his voice drawling like a true Louisiana man. "Heck, we probably saved the FBI a whole bunch of paperwork. These two fellas were probably low-level drones anyway. NSA might've known about 'em, but they probably have bigger fish to fry overseas. If anybody's gonna have a problem with it, it'll likely be the EPA. Like I said before, it ain't my favorite thing to go dumpin' in the ocean, but you know what they say about desperate times."

"Troy," I said. "You saved my life, you know that, right?"

"To be fair, Mr. Thackerson," he said, tipping his cowboy hat back on his head. "I was mostly thinking about saving mine."

I couldn't help but laugh. I really liked this guy.

"I wish you coulda met Martha," I said. "You two would've made fast friends. And Victoria, too. I'd love for you to meet her. I'm worried about her, Troy."

"I know you are, sir," he said, as traffic inched along.

The sun was in our eyes when we finally crossed over onto Key West. Troy turned onto Roosevelt and acted like he knew where he was headed. I asked him, and he said he knew a couple of good people who might be able to help.

11

SHAMELESS
DAVID BERENS

A FEW MINUTES LATER, we pulled into the A&B Marina.

"Where are we, Troy?" I asked as he slid into a spot.

"You'll see," he said, helping me out of the truck.

Troy introduced me to Sully Pratt Armand and his wife, Rosa. Sully was a big, beefy guy with a gray chin beard that almost reached his belly button. I could tell because Sully wore a bright red Hawaiian shirt that might have been three sizes too small and hung open on his brutish frame. He thrust a Corona and a shot of something into our hands as we walked up. I thought about turning it down, but a tweak in my elbow made me think a quick shot and a beer might make me feel a little better. The beer was ice cold and the shot was surprisingly smooth.

Rosa was the opposite of Sully in many respects. She reminded me of Victoria. She was slender, dark-haired, and Brazilian. This I could tell because she wore a small blouse fashioned from a bandanna-sized Brazilian flag.

Like most people in Key West, Sully worked three different jobs, four if you counted his not-so-legit cigar business. Rosa only worked two. She was a daytime bartender at Alonzo's Oyster Bar and at night she hosted at Dreamgirls. When she told me this, I pulled out the folded neon sheet of paper and asked her about Victoria. I realized looking at it this time, there was a hostess in the background of the picture. I looked at Rosa, then looked at Troy. He winked. He had known Rosa was on the flier the whole time, and that's why he'd brought us here.

"Oh yeah," she said. "Shame! I love her. She's so cute and innocent. I tried to tell her early on that she could make a ton of money down at the Pink Panty, but she's too good for that place."

Rosa suddenly looked embarrassed, realizing that she had revealed to Victoria's father that she had suggested stripping as a way to make money. Troy did a spit-take with his beer, but I just shrugged. It had crossed my mind that she might be doing something like this to make ends meet.

"Rosa, it's okay. I'm an adult and Victoria is too. Though it's not a choice I would've wanted her to make, she's doing the best she can with what she has. When Martha and I brought her into our family, we only wanted the best for her. And now I feel as if I've let her down ..."

The flood gates opened. I was spilling it all out on the dock. I trailed off, not sure why I was telling all this to a complete stranger. But Rosa grabbed me and hugged me, squeezing me as the tears streamed down my cheeks.

"It's okay, Papa," she said, wiping my face. "We gonna get your girl back for you. Come sit at the bar. I'll text Shame, er, Victoria, and let her know we coming."

"No, no," I said. "Please don't. I don't want to surprise her, but I don't want her to ..."

"You don't want her to run away again," Rosa said. "I understand."

Rosa looked down at her watch. "Come. Sit with me at the bar at Alonzo's. I got fifteen minutes on this shift, then Sully gonna take me to Dreamgirls. We'll go together."

Again, my mind rebelled. *No. I'm going now*, I thought.

"Thank you so much," I said. "But I really need to get there quicker than that. There are men, very bad men, who are after her. I don't know why, but there were two of them on—"

I had been about to relay the events of this morning, but Troy grabbed my arm and squeezed just tight enough to make me realize that Rosa and Sully didn't really need to know all of that.

"Harvey," Troy said quietly. I realized it was the first time he had called me by my first name. "Fifteen minutes ain't gonna make a difference."

He nodded slightly toward Alonzo's, and Rosa got the message. She smiled, patted me on the shoulder, and walked away.

"Those men, this morning," Troy said, "probably found you by tracking Victoria's phone. And that phone is now completely off the grid, if you catch my drift. It ain't likely they have any idea where your girl is. So, let's take a load off, we've been goin' ninety to nothin' since before the sun came up. Sully and Rosa are good people. Let them help you like I've helped you."

I took a slow, deep breath. "You're right, Troy. You're right."

He clucked his teeth and tipped his hat. "It ain't often, but it does happen once in a blue moon."

"I don't even know what that means, but it makes me feel a little better about this whole thing."

We walked around to sit at the bar at Alonzo's. Rosa screamed at a soccer game on the television. Drunk tourists stared at her every time she bent over, and Sully winked as they stuffed big wads of money into her tip jar.

I ordered a bourbon instead of a beer. Troy got another Corona. Rosa offered another shot, but I turned this one down. I wanted to be clear-headed when I saw Victoria. In fifteen minutes, warm bourbon swirling around in my tummy, I felt I was ready. What I wasn't ready for, was for Sully to come jogging around the corner pulling a rickshaw. He already had a slight sheen of sweat on his forehead, and I wondered how fast we would be able to go in the contraption. I started to voice my concern and suggest a taxi, but Troy assured me this was the best way.

As we meandered our way over to Duval Street, I began to understand why. Traffic was hindered by the constant flow of tourists and locals wandering back and forth across the street. And when we reached Sloppy Joe's, the street was barricaded, blocking motorized vehicles. Troy tried to explain that there was some festival going on, but I couldn't hear him over the cacophony of music and voices and sounds all around us.

"Why not just go one street over?" I asked Rosa, who was putting on heavy makeup, preparing for her shift.

"Not allowed," she said, wagging a finger. She patted my knee. "Don't worry, Papa. This is the best way."

I decided that I would take their word for it. When in Rome ...

12

SHAMELESS
DAVID BERENS

WE BEGAN to wind our way through the masses past the tourist-driven bars at the north end of town. As we got closer to Dreamgirls, the music played a bit louder, but it was my kind of music. Big bands and crooners and songbirds from the fifties and sixties. I also noticed the people walking around became more ... flamboyant. Some wore outlandish costumes with feathers and sequins like Vegas showgirls. Some wore costumes that seemed to have some secret innuendo portrayed on them. Some were topless or even naked, with only body paint as clothing. All were smiling and happy and bouncing around like they didn't have a care in the world.

I was startled to see Cher, Marilyn, and Rita standing on the street handing out the same yellow flier, urging people to enter the amateur contest. When Cher caught sight of us—or more precisely, when she saw Troy—she came wobbling over awkwardly in her impossibly high stilettos and grabbed him by the arm.

"Baby doll," she said, licking her lips in a very Cher-esque manner, "I knew you couldn't stay away."

She pulled Troy from the rickshaw and we all followed. Before I could react, Troy was dragged away from us as we walked into Dreamgirls. My heart leaped as I saw a dark-haired young woman behind the hostess stand, but when she looked up, it was clear she was a drag queen. Her name tag read "Mariah," and yes, she was a convincing lookalike for the '80's songstress. Looking beyond her, all I could see was a dark hallway. I'll be honest, I wasn't impressed at first. Everything was black and industrial and plain. It was a stark contrast to the rainbow of color we had just seen outside.

"I'm looking for Shame," I said to Mariah.

"Baby, you won't find any shame here," she said, and my anxiety flared until I realized she didn't know what I meant.

"No, you don't understand," I said. "My daughter works here. Her name is Shame. Well, her name is Victoria, but I suppose she goes by Shame when she's working."

I pointed to one of the fliers hanging on the wall. "That's her, the dark-haired girl in the—"

Someone grabbed my arm and ushered us past the hostess stand down a dark hallway. I looked and saw that it was Rita Hayworth.

"These beautiful people are with us, darling," Rita called over her shoulder. "Come on in, sugar. Let's get you a seat."

"But ... but ... I need to find my girl," I said.

Rita flashed a smirk at Sully and Rosa. "Not sure you'll find her in here, darling. But what you will find is a show that will knock your socks off."

She led us around the hall and when we turned the corner, everything changed. The walls were draped with curtains of every color, like festival tapestries. The lights dimmed and fairy lights began to shine and twinkle all around us. Rita sat us at a bar top table near the stage and Rosa went backstage to start her shift. A spotlight shone through the darkness as the opening chords of "I Got You, Babe" echoed around us. Cher was amazing. She pulled some young fella up on stage to play the part of Sonny Bono. He was thoroughly and completely flustered by the time she was through with him.

She finished to thunderous applause and cheering, then began to lay out the details of the contest. I didn't hear much of it as I scanned the crowd, searching for Victoria. I would have walked around the place looking for her, but it was too crowded. Within minutes, the first contestant was ushered out on stage and the night got wild.

I couldn't make out any faces in the darkness, but as any parent will tell you, they know their child, day or night. An hour went by, and we saw embarrassed and not-so-embarrassed dancers take the stage in what basically amounted to drag karaoke.

And then it was Troy's turn.

13

SHAMELESS
DAVID BERENS

A TWANGY ELECTRIC guitar began a thrumming rhythm, and the crowd was suddenly on their feet. It was not a song I recognized, but the lyrics suggested that one could save a horse by riding a cowboy. And tonight, my new friend Troy Bodean fulfilled that role.

Women and men alike seemed drawn to his not-so-polished way of swinging his hips around as he tipped his hat to all of them. To my surprise, some of the other drag performers took the stage with him —totally against the rules of the competition. They, like the members of the audience, were swept up in Troy's performance.

Cher wrapped a glittering silver feather boa around his neck and Marilyn gathered the dollar bills strewn about the stage. I was mesmerized, too. But as the final chorus began to fade, I remembered what I was doing here.

I tapped Sully—who was whistling loudly for Troy—on the shoulder. "I don't think she's here. I haven't seen her all night. What's going on? Can you find Rosa and see if she knows what's happening?"

He nodded and got up from the table. I was alone. I was surrounded by happy, party people, and I was alone. Out of nowhere, Troy sat down at the table, his face covered by an exuberant smile. He had a light sheen of sweat on his forehead.

"Can you believe it?" he said.

"What's that, Troy?"

He slapped five one-hundred-dollar bills on the table. "I won the whole dang thing. Apparently, these folks appreciate the finer qualities of Big 'n Rich. Who knew? And would ya believe it, I'm qualified to enter the next round which is going to be held in ..."

His voice trailed off. I started to cry.

"You didn't find her, did you?"

I shook my head. "She's not here. Rosa went backstage. Then I sent Sully after her, but neither of them has come back. Something's wrong, Troy. I don't know what, but something is wrong. I'm going to see if I can get around to the back of the building. Surely, they'll let her father see her."

"Okay," he said. "Let's get around there and see if—"

I put my hand on his shoulder. "No. You get back to Shark Key. That fella, what's his name ... Chuck. Chuck will be looking for his Wagoneer. Besides, I can take it from here. This is something I gotta do on my own."

I reached into my pocket and pulled out the key to the boat. The floating keychain Martha had bought for me dangled from it. A single, scripted word was printed along the side: *Serendipity*. I slid it across the table to Troy. His mouth hung open and he looked from the key to the money he'd just won.

I winked at him and he handed me the five hundred dollars, just as we had agreed out on the boat earlier today. I folded it and put it into my shirt pocket.

"*Serendipity* indeed," I said.

I made my way through the room and down the dark hallway back toward the hostess stand. As I rounded the corner, I could see out the glass door to Duval Street. It was the only glass on the front of the building. I froze. I only saw a shadow pass by, but as I said before, a parent knows their child, day or night. And I knew that shadow was my Vic.

PART II

CHRIS NILES

Chris(tine) Niles has been telling stories since she was a lying kid. Now she's figuring out how to make a career of it. Because she likes to eat, she tried for about fifteen minutes to write romance. But her characters kept killing each other, so she switched to thrillers. Her heart is buried deep in the hammock north of Sugarloaf Key, and you can only find it from a kayak. Despite that, her body lives in northeastern Indiana with her husband, two adult daughters, and a hungry four-legged sack of fur named Franklin.
Visit chrisnilesbooks.com to learn more about Chris' Shark Key Adventures and to download the free novella, *Lost Palm*.

14

SHAMELESS
CHRIS NILES

I SPRINTED DOWN THE HALL.

Well, sprint might be a strong word for an arthritic old fart who'd already taken two spills in one day. So it wasn't altogether surprising when I felt a heavy hand on my shoulder. But nothing was going to keep me from following my girl. I shook it off as I heard a smooth, deep voice behind me.

"Mr. Thackerson."

I kept moving.

"Harvey. I can help."

Maybe it was tunnel vision, or maybe it was just that the walls of the narrow hallway were painted black, but all I could see was the glass door and the thick river of humans flowing past it.

I shoved my way out into the crowd and began to push my way upstream.

"Victoria. Vic, honey. Wait up!"

I screamed into the crowd until my voice grew hoarse, following the shadow of my daughter. I could feel her presence, but that also meant I felt her slipping further away. I finally stopped, dropped to a bench, and tried to catch my breath. Music blared, and a distinctly sweet, skunky scent hung in the thick salt air. The throng of people pulled my attention to the street. And then my jaw dropped.

In my tunnel vision trying to catch up to Victoria, I hadn't really taken in the details of the crowd. My gaze snapped up to a garish banner stretched high across Duval Street.

WELCOME TO FANTASY FEST

Below the sign, hundreds of humans in varying states of undress streamed down the street. I'm no prude, but I can't say I'd ever seen so much skin and body paint and leather straps. But my girl was already across the street and the more I gawked, the further she got from me. I pushed through a cluster of sunburned tourists and caught a glimpse of the back of her head. The thick black hair I had braided in the mornings as I stood behind her at the breakfast table while Martha scrambled eggs and buttered toast.

And then she dodged ahead of a tall woman covered in vibrant body paint and disappeared from my sight.

"Victoria!" I shouted, but my voice was drowned out in the din of the crowd.

I pushed on, fighting my way down block after block. But as the crowd grew thicker, I lost sight of my daughter. The adrenaline faded and I drifted with the crowd until the current spit me out into a narrow alley where the stench of piss hung in the humid, stagnant air and thumping music echoed off the bare brick. I inched as close to the street as I could without getting caught up again in the flow of humanity. Desperate for some untainted air, I traded piss for sweat and sunscreen, sucked in a breath, and made for the next block over.

The channel released me into the fresh air of a shaded street. The sidewalk was barely wide enough for me to hobble past white picket fences covered in bougainvillea and waist-high, crumbling concrete walls guarding lush tropical gardens. Finally, those gave way to an open porch, its gingerbread railing inviting me to collapse against it and find support. I flung myself down on the second step and tried to catch my breath.

When my tunnel vision receded and I could lift my head, I gazed up and down the block. Cars lined the opposite curb, each bumper kissing the next, squeezed so tight I couldn't see how they'd ever free themselves. At the intersections at both ends of the block, clusters of folks made their way toward the party. I was the only one, it seemed, who was trying to get away.

Had that even been Victoria? It had to have been. I knew her like I knew my own reflection. But why would she run from me? Why didn't she stop when she heard her name? My voice?

I had to dive back in. I couldn't give up now. But I had a foreboding sense that my search for her was just beginning.

I wrapped my fingers around the banister and heaved my aching body to my feet. I took a few steps, warming up the joints that had already started to stiffen, and started back toward the party.

I found a pocket and slipped back into the crowd on Duval, moving more slowly now. As I adjusted to the idea that I'd lost Victoria, I started to see more of the depravity around me. I stopped—a boulder in the river of people creating an eddy around my frozen form—and stared. A moment later, I felt a large but gentle hand nudge my jaw closed, and then that same low voice resonated in my ear.

"Harvey. We care about your daughter, too. Let us help you."

I slowly turned. Beside me stood one of the biggest women I'd ever seen. She towered over me, her broad shoulders and solid waist separated by a tiny white bandeau top barely covering a chest that couldn't be natural, considering the Adam's apple that bobbed as she spoke.

"I'm Kara. I own Dreamgirls. Your daughter's been working at my club for a few weeks. She called herself Shame, but it was obvious that wasn't her real name. Around here, we try to let people keep their secrets as long as they need to. But when trouble finds them, we do what we can to help. One Human Family and all. So come on back with me. We'll see what we need to do next."

15

SHAMELESS
CHRIS NILES

THE PERSON CALLING herself Kara set a steaming cup of coffee in front of me, then she lowered herself into a chair and took my hand in hers. Now, I'm not a big guy, but I'm not slight. In the slightest. But in her hand, mine looked almost like a child's. A wrinkly child, but still a child.

I looked from my pale hand held in her dark one to meet her eyes. Between two perfectly symmetrical and sharply drawn eyebrows, her skin pulled into two parallel furrows. She leaned across the table and gripped my hand even tighter.

"Like I told you out there, she told us her name was Shame. Last time any of us saw her was the night before last," she began.

I felt my shoulders tighten, and Kara loosened her grip on my hand and nudged the coffee cup toward me. As I lifted it to my lips, the dark elixir sloshed and spilled over the edges. I raised my other hand and clutched the mug like a toddler holding a sippy cup. A moment I had never been able to watch with Victoria.

So many moments I'd missed.

Martha used to joke about how we skipped the messiest parts of parenting—the diaper blowouts and three-in-the-morning feedings and spit-up on our Sunday best. But we also missed her first steps. First birthday smash-cake. Her first day of school.

Sure, we still had enjoyed a few. First date. Prom night. Her first time behind the wheel of a car—that one nearly gave Martha a heart attack. But there were still so many parts of Victoria's life that we simply weren't a part of. And now that she was missing? Now that I didn't know how—or if—I would ever see her again? I clutched those remembered moments like an addict. They were all I had to hold onto, and nothing else mattered.

I took a sip of the coffee, and my head jerked back at the jolt of sweetness.

"It's for the shock, sugar." Kara's soothing voice pulled my attention back to her presence. "The Brits' answer to any crisis is tea, but I just can't see a cup of Earl Gray in a place like this." She waved that massive hand around.

The club was empty except for the performers milling around near the back dressing room, changing into street clothes, and murmuring softly among themselves with just an occasional glance toward us. Bright fluorescent lights tucked against the dark industrial ceiling illuminated black-painted girders and ventilation ducts, their shadows falling on the upturned stools and tall bar tables. The bartender slowly made his way around the floor, swaying with his mop to some tune only he heard.

I sipped the coffee. Although it made my teeth ache, my nerves began to settle, and with each sip, the cup shook a bit less. Finally, I set it on the table and looked back up at Kara.

"Shame?"

She nodded. "I knew it wasn't the name her mama gave her. Most of the girls do that, at least at first." Her chin tipped toward the little group in the back. As they started to drift toward us, I realized that about half the performers were men, and the other half were women. Or at least they looked like women. As they drew closer, I spotted tell-tale Adam's apples on a few. And if I was being honest, they were the prettier ones. Girls I'd be proud to introduce as my daughter.

"They don't use their real names?"

"I didn't say that." She sucked in a deep breath, and her eyes flicked up to the ceiling before they dropped back to meet mine. "Honey, the name you're given sometimes isn't who you really are. I started out as Carlos. Do I look anything like a Carlos?"

She winked at me and waved her arms up and down her, uh, ample torso. Could I say that these days? Call a woman's body "ample"? I didn't know what was okay and what wasn't anymore. But that was the first word I thought of when my eyes landed on more cleavage than I thought most women liked to show these days.

A soft giggle spilled from her lips. "I see what you're thinking. It's okay. I paid a lot for these, so I like when you appreciate them."

I shrugged. "Ya never know these days. And I've learned a lot having a daughter. I'd rather be respectful than, you know ..."

Her face darkened. "Your daughter is a good girl who's just got a problem that's bigger than her. I don't know what's going on. She didn't open up and tell me much. She kept to herself, mostly. But I got a little bit out of her in bits and pieces."

I perked up. "You did?"

"A little." She paused. Her eyes flicked beyond my shoulder and she gave a little nod, then turned back to me. "First, I know she loves you and her mom."

At the mention of my late wife, I flinched, all too aware that neither of my girls was here with me. My chest tightened to fill the black hole at my core.

Kara waited until the silence forced more words from my lips.

"Her mother died not too long ago. Nothing was right after that. Victoria locked herself away and wouldn't talk to me at all."

"I'm so sorry."

"Thanks." I shrugged. "Funny memory. In the first couple of days after Martha was gone, people said that to us a lot, as you can imagine. And as they'd say it to Victoria, she'd stiffen up and I could just tell she was fighting to hold something in. Until one woman from our church came up to us at the funeral. Vic and I both knew her—she was a horrible, backstabbing woman. Always nice to your face, but the minute you turned around, she was saying the worst things about everyone. Anyway, she came up and started telling Victoria what a wonderful woman Martha was, and as she closed with the inevitable 'I'm sorry,' Vic burst out, 'Your *sorry* doesn't help me.' Her eyes bugged out like even she was surprised at what she'd just said."

Feeling exhausted, I pulled my lips into a smile. "The woman was horrified, but I couldn't feel bad at all. I just burst out laughing. It was the first time I'd laughed since the second Martha died. That was the moment I thought we'd be okay, me and Vic. We'd get through this together. But when I opened my eyes, I saw her flying through the door at the back of the fellowship hall, and I was left there all by myself."

"That must have felt so lonely."

"You have no idea."

"I might. I've had my share of losses, honey. We all have. And sometimes it's a loss even when they're still here. The person you love is still alive, but they just shut you out."

I looked up at this person I didn't know at all, this person who just a day ago I would have thought of as some kind of aberration, and I felt like she knew me. She understood things about me I hadn't even known. And it terrified me.

I pulled my hand from hers, dropped it into my lap, and began picking the cuticle on my thumb. I rubbed my tender elbow. I took an awkward sip of coffee, and my eyes darted around the room.

Kara sat back in her chair and I felt the breath rush back into my lungs through the space between us. The bartender slid up to the table and set a coffee cup beside her, then turned to me and shook the glass pot. I nodded, and without a word, he splashed the steaming brown goodness to the brim, then disappeared behind me.

Kara took a sip. "Shame—Victoria—turned up here a couple weeks ago. She told me she needed to make some cash, quick." One carefully drawn eyebrow rose as her face twisted into what looked like sadness, and she gave a cynical shrug. "I hear that a lot. More than I'd like. Most people who turn up down here are running from something, so I've learned to not ask a lot of questions. I figure my purpose in the world is to give people a spot to rest their worries, get their feet back under them, and figure out what's next without me judging them or making their life any harder. So that's what I did for her. I accepted whatever she wanted to tell me, and I hoped she'd figure out she could be safe here."

I slumped in my chair. "I'm not sure she can be safe anywhere."

Kara's head tilted to the side.

"Look, Vic didn't run because her mom died or because we had some kind of fight. We would have gotten through it." I looked down at the coffee swirling in my cup, unsure if I should say more. But this woman just felt safe.

"We adopted her when she was eleven. But before that, she saw ... " I fumbled for the right words. "She saw some things no kid should have to see. And the, uh ... the perpetrators of those, uh ..." I trailed off, not even knowing how to explain the hell that had brought Victoria into witness protection in the first place, let alone how much of it was safe to share.

When it became clear I wasn't going to say anything more, Kara sat forward in her chair and squared her wide shoulders.

"Alrighty, then. So we're looking at something altogether different here. And now that I understand, I know just the person to help. You just sip that coffee and hang tight."

I glanced down at my watch. It was nearly 1 a.m. Who answers the phone at that hour?

16

SHAMELESS
CHRIS NILES

DESPITE DRINKING a third cup of over-sugared coffee that appeared in my hands at some point, I finally had just drifted to sleep, my forehead resting on my good arm. It reminded me of how Victoria would fall asleep at her desk when she was supposed to be studying trigonometry.

She always said numbers put her to sleep. That she needed history or literature to keep her awake. People doing things. That's what interested her, she said. Not "abstract" things like numbers or dates.

"How are numbers or dates abstract?" I'd ask her. They seemed like the most concrete, real things in the world to me.

Then she'd reply. "What does 1492 look like, Harvey?"

She always called me Harvey when she wanted to get under my skin or make a point. In fact, when we adopted her, it took a year before the first time she called me "Dad." And even then, it wasn't often. She usually avoided calling me anything at all.

But the child had a point.

"We can look at portraits of Christopher Columbus," she explained. "I have illustrations of his ships. The maps the explorers made. We can see how the maps changed the more they explored, and we can read the stories they told as they met different cultures and people over time. I can track with that. I can see them like they're movies. But the lines and curves of numbers that represent a date without any stories attached? Just puts me to sleep."

Then she'd flip a page in her math book, drop her forehead back on the page, and start snoring.

Teenagers.

A heavy hand on my shoulder pulled me back to the brightly lit room. A fresh coffee sat by my arm, and I felt the presence of a small group of people behind Kara. I glanced around. All the performers had left, and the bartender hovered in the shadows like some kind of guardian angel.

I took a sip of coffee, then creaked to my feet, my joints stiff and my arm sore from the long day of bumps and bruises my poor old body wasn't used to. A blonde woman with short, curly hair stretched her hand out to me. At her left side, a German shepherd sat with his unblinking eyes trained on me.

"I'm Kate. Kate Kingbury. I, uh ..." She glanced at Kara, then back to me. "I find things. And people. I find ... that's it, I guess. I find." She motioned toward the dog. "And this is Whiskey."

I shook her hand as she waved to the people with her.

"Well, we find."

The tall Black woman beside her tucked a laptop under her left arm and reached out to me with her right. "I'm Michelle. I'm the geek."

She settled in across the table from me and snapped the laptop open while a man with sandy hair, a close-trimmed beard, and a torso that could barely squeeze into a T-shirt introduced himself.

"I'm Tony. I kick doors." His grin was contagious, and I couldn't help but feel like he did a lot more than that as he gave me a firm handshake that clearly could have broken all my fingers if he'd wanted to. I spotted the edge of a tattoo peeking out of the sleeve of his T-shirt. I started to ask, but I watched as his eyes tracked mine to his shoulder and back again, his expression darkening by the second.

"Nice to meet you, Tony." I settled on that, his expression telling me what I didn't need to ask.

I looked back to the blonde, Kate. She looked familiar. In fact, they all looked like I'd seen them before.

"You've been staying at Shark Key, haven't you?"

Tony's question snapped their faces into context for me. Of course. I'd seen them all up on the restaurant deck just the night before, which felt like a month ago.

"I have. Got in a few days ago." I looked from face to face, all so different, but all showing the same open expression. I'd only just met them, but I somehow knew I could trust them to help me find Victoria. I just didn't know where to start. I couldn't tell the whole story again.

Kate nodded toward my chair, then settled into the one across the table and saved me from having to decide. "I can't imagine how difficult this must be for you, Harvey. I need to ask you a few questions, and I need you to be as honest as you can. If you don't know the answers, it's better to tell me that than to make something up. Every detail could be important, but the false ones are worse than nothing at all."

I nodded at her unusual introduction, and I answered some very basic details like Victoria's legal name, birthdate, and our adoption date. Michelle's fingers flew across her keyboard, and the woman fell into a screen-trance as Kate and Tony continued the conversation.

They asked questions like, "How often did you see her before she disappeared?" And "Did you know most of her friends?"

Questions that made me realize how little I knew my barely-grown-up daughter.

The textbooks say that teenagers need to "individuate." At least that's what Martha told me. That they need to figure out who they are away from their parents. To make their own decisions and make a few mistakes. So I thought I was giving her the space to do that. But I was so ashamed now, I didn't want to answer those questions.

"I was a good dad. We were good parents. We tried to let her have her privacy—"

"Mr. Thackerson, wait." Michelle's hand flew up and she interrupted without taking her eyes off the screen. She tapped a few more keys, furrowed her brow, looked up at Kate. Then her gaze settled on me.

My head fell into my hands as she dropped the bomb.

"Why didn't you start with WitSec?"

I slumped. Thought. Then I straightened up. It took all the energy I had left to straighten my spine and summon the strength I needed to defend my choice. With a joke.

"The first rule of WitSec is, don't talk about WitSec?"

Great delivery there, Harv.

No one laughed.

Michelle raised an eyebrow and tried again. "I can read the record. Or you can tell us. Your choice."

My eyes darted around. My joke wasn't a lie. I wasn't supposed to talk about it. Ever. Not even with Vic. When you have a secret that everyone knows but no one talks about, they say it's an elephant in the room, right? This wasn't an elephant. This was a brontosaurus. It was supposed to be extinct, but it just kept coming back.

Kate leaned forward on her elbows, her expression much kinder than Michelle's surprised scowl. Her voice was barely above a whisper and I strained to hear it over the whoosh of the air conditioning.

"Harvey, I'm sure you're scared. I get it. Witness security doesn't get put in place when the stakes are low. If your daughter was under long-term protection, then that changes everything. She didn't just run away, did she?"

I felt like the spine I'd just found was melting away like hot Jell-O.

"I keep hoping, maybe ..." I felt Kara's hand on my shoulder, and it infused enough strength for me to keep talking. "She ran, yes. I wanted to believe it wasn't connected. That she just wanted to find herself after her mom died. But then this morning ..."

All three of them stared at me. Michelle's eyes flared, then she dropped her attention back to her laptop.

"You can tell us."

I tried to place Tony's accent. He hadn't said more than twenty words, but it was distinctive. Southern, but yet ... not.

I didn't even know where to start. The beginning? This morning? There was no way I was willing to put Troy in jeopardy, so I needed some time to edit. So, the very beginning. A very good place to start. Like Maria in the musical that the girls wanted to watch every Christmas.

"I can only tell you what they told me. Victoria has never talked about it."

That was the truth.

"Her father worked for one of the alphabet agencies, and he was involved in that big case where they were trying to take down a bunch of cartels in Mexico." I wasn't really sure how much detail was appropriate, so I tried to keep it vague. "It didn't go well for him."

I stopped for a sip of my coffee, mainly to buy time. Watch their reactions.

Michelle caught Tony's eyes. "Sandoval."

He turned back to me. "They took her?"

"She escaped. Her parents weren't so lucky."

"Poor kid." Kate buried her face in her hands.

"She never talked about it. Refused to go to therapy. Just said she wanted to look forward. Like she'd taken her whole past and locked it in a vault."

"So what changed?"

"Everything, I guess." I shrugged, racking my brain for specifics. "She graduated college. Martha died. She got that damned letter. I don't know. A few months ago, I thought her future was looking bright. Filled with possibility. I thought she'd put it all behind her."

"Wait, what letter?"

"It seemed like nothing, really. Just some garbage from what we thought was a supremacist. We gave it to the cops and they said it was nothing. But she was skittish after that." I shrugged. "Martha and I were planning a big trip. We bought the boat and had everything mapped out to come down here. To Shark Key. It looked like a perfect place for a new start. Victoria hadn't really found her footing as an adult, so we wanted to show her something different. Someplace she could see the sun."

Kara lowered herself into the chair beside me more gracefully than I thought anyone that size could.

"She mentioned being 'on her own again' but she didn't ..."

I felt a flush in my cheeks. "It was probably a mistake, but we didn't include her in the planning. I wanted to surprise her. I guess maybe she overheard us talking about it and thought we were going to leave without her. And then we lost Martha. So when Vic disappeared, I thought she was just trying to leave me before I left her. The therapists say that's a thing for a kid who's lost ... everything."

Kara patted my hand, and Tony finally broke the silence.

"Did the police go back to the letter after your daughter disappeared?"

I shook my head. "I had a photo of it, but my phone's on the bottom of the Gulf."

Michelle's cheek ticked up. In the time it took me to drain my coffee cup, she had found her way into what she called "the cloud" and found every photo I thought I'd ever taken with my phone. I felt hopeful and violated all at the same time.

Tony grabbed the laptop and zoomed in on the letter.

"Kate, look."

She shook her head and he pointed. "This symbol. It's faint, but do you think your Brighton Beach buddy could help?"

He tapped the screen and a second later, her phone dinged. She punched out a quick message and then dropped her phone back to the table. "Guess we'll see."

Tony turned back to me. "That was more than just a random racist, wasn't it?"

I nodded. But I wasn't ready to tell them about my call from Cunningham this morning.

"Kara, has there been anyone suspicious hanging around the club in the last few days?"

"Not that I've noticed." She waved over to the bar. "Paul? C'mere a sec?" Her hands fluttered in the air as she hollered.

The giant bouncer I'd seen earlier came over. Kara's hands flew again as she spoke and I realized she was signing.

"Did you see anyone hanging around? Watching Shame in particular? The new girl?"

He paused for a second, his blue eyes drifting toward the ceiling, then flaring with recognition. He looked in her eye and signed back, his head nodding.

It took what felt like ten minutes for my heart to start beating again. I thought maybe they were going to have to helicopter me to a trauma center in Miami, but Victoria needed me here to find her, so ... mind over matter, right?

Paul's description of the two men he'd spotted lurking around and had thrown out of the club just the day before matched the details of the two men Troy had, uh, "taken care of" in the cabin of my boat this morning.

This morning? It seemed so long ago. So much had happened since then.

I didn't quite know how to tell these kind folks that not only did I know who those men were, but that I'd watched them both die by the hand of their Amateur Night winner.

As I was forming a plausible story in my head, Kate's phone buzzed. She snatched it up, then waggled it in front of Tony before handing it to Michelle.

"Got it."

As Michelle's fingers flew across her keyboard again, Kate filled me in.

"Definitely Sandoval. I suppose that isn't news to you, but Vova gave me a name." She ticked her head toward her friend, typing furiously.

I reached for my cup. My hands shook as I sipped, and then the cup dropped from my hands, too tired and achy to grip it. Whiskey jumped to his feet. Coffee spilled across the table, and Tony leaped up as it dripped over the edge nearest to him.

Paul appeared with a wet bar towel, and Kara pushed to her feet and held her hand out to me.

"Look, Harvey, it's late and you're exhausted. It'll take a while for Michelle to chase this down, so how about I take you upstairs to my apartment? You can clean up and get a little sleep while we figure out our next move."

17

SHAMELESS
CHRIS NILES

I AWOKE WITH A START.

Weak light seeped past the blinds that hung behind the colorful, gauzy fabric curtains. I sat up, the hairs on my arms standing on end, and rubbed my eyes. Kara's bedroom looked like a Mardi Gras parade had thrown up all over the room. Jewel-toned chaos in gauze and velvet and beads and mirrors. My toes dug into the thick rug and I almost relaxed. Until—

POP POP POP

The three sharp sounds came from beneath my feet.

Then barking echoed from below me. Another pop, and almost simultaneously, the rug under my feet exploded in a burst of splinters and shaggy fibers.

I scrambled off the bed and across the apartment, as far away as possible from the damaged area. Another two shots splintered the floor in the center of the room. I bolted through the bathroom door and climbed into the cast-iron clawfoot tub.

Good thing, too.

A barrage of shots plowed through the floor and into the bottom of the mattress where I'd just been sleeping.

"I guess they found the Sandoval guys," I muttered.

I stood up long enough to pull two thick, purple bath sheets from the towel bar. Then I made myself a little nest, pulled the shower curtain closed, and cowered in the tub as the muffled battle ended in a flurry that sounded like the grand finale of a fireworks show.

After a few minutes of silence, I heard footsteps on the stairs. The hinges on the apartment door creaked. My heart pounded so loud I heard it echoing against the white enameled tub.

"Harvey?"

Kara's voice scared me out of my skin.

"Harvey, are you up here? Where—oh, my God, MY RUG!"

I took three deep breaths, holding them at the top, then fighting to release them as I counted to eight and my heart slowed to a countable rate.

When I finally could speak, I replied, "You're more worried about your rug than there might be the same holes in my body?"

Kara filled the open bathroom door, blocking the little bit of light that had made it into the small, windowless room. "I checked for blood first ..." She breezed into the room as if she hadn't just survived a freaking gun battle down below. Reached into the tub and pulled me to my feet. My elbow screamed in protest.

She led me to a stool in her kitchen, popped a plastic pod into the single-use coffee maker on the counter, and pressed a button.

"So as you might have guessed by now, we didn't have to go looking. Sandoval's guys came to us."

"I gathered. How did all that escape the attention of law enforcement? It sounded like the Battle of Mariupol down there!"

She pulled the full cup from the machine. "The club is soundproofed. We run shows till 2 a.m. on the weekends, and even though the rest of the neighborhood is hopping, too, some people actually do live around here, so we try to keep our noise contained. Anyway, we got Sandoval's guys, but it won't be long before they send more. It sounds like your girl saw some pretty serious shit." She leveled a serious gaze at me.

"Harvey, we need to know what we're up against. If you haven't noticed, we can handle ourselves pretty well. And we've got more backup. But you're hiding something big and I need to know what it is." She dumped three spoons of sugar into the coffee and planted it on the marble counter in front of me. "Spill it."

So I did.

Twenty minutes and another coffee later, Kara and I descended the stairs.

Tied to chairs on the stage with spotlights trained on them were two Hispanic men dressed in black. They were positioned back-to-back but separated by about four feet. At the edge of the stage, directly between them, Kate's huge dog, Whiskey, sat at attention.

The smaller of the two men shifted in his seat. The dog's hind legs rose halfway, his hair stood on end, and a deep growl resonated in his chest. The man dropped his chin back to his chest, whispering, "I'm sorry, dog. Sorry."

The dog ended his growl with a single, sharp bark, then sat back down and resumed his watch.

As I walked past, I realized a leg of the man's black tactical pants was in tatters, and blood trickled down his skin in a bite-shaped pattern. But the punctures weren't deep. Clearly, the dog had done his job with more restraint than I would have shown.

Across the room, my new friends sat around a table. Two long, black guns lay on its surface. As I approached them, Tony reached up and adjusted a bandage wrapped around Kate's upper arm.

"What happened? If this is—"

"It's okay, Harvey. This was nothing. Really."

"I'm so sorry to have dragged you into this. Look, we should just call the Marshal. I don't have his number, but he contacted me yesterday." I threw a glance toward Michelle and furrowed my brows into a question.

She shook her head. "I've been through your call log."

Kate dropped her forearms on the table, her hands clenched into fists. "More importantly, though, we've been through your daughter's call history. And either you're still keeping something from us, or she was keeping something from you. So which is it, Mr. Thackerson?"

My heart thumped as my brain scrambled to figure out what she could be talking about. Victoria had been distant for a while, and we knew less and less of her life as she progressed at BC, but we had always tried to make sure we knew her friends and at least the rough outline of what was going on in her life.

"She had some things that were private, sure. Doesn't every girl? But keeping important stuff from me? I don't think—"

"Harvey." She waited until I met her stare. "There are calls and texts going back months."

"Calls? With who?"

I thought I heard Michelle mumble "Whom," but Kate's answer yanked me back into focus.

"Rico Mendoza. Sandoval's second-in-command."

I couldn't breathe. Victoria had been talking to the men who had killed her parents?

"What? For how long? Were they threatening her?"

Kate glanced over at Tony, then at Michelle, then back to me. All three of them looked ... concerned. Finally, Kate answered.

"He wasn't threatening her, Harvey. He's dating her."

"Dating?"

"Well," Tony drawled, "whatever it is that kids do these days. Talking, I think they call it? One of the last messages, they agreed to meet up."

Kate ticked her chin toward him.

He hesitated. "The day before yesterday."

"I had her phone. I didn't see any texts."

Michelle's face softened. "Harvey, she had a second phone, and the calls and messages continued after she left Boston. People do that sometimes when they've got something to hide. Look, I can't tell what they talked about, but from the texts, it doesn't look like she knew who he was. There's no mention of Sandoval or the business or what happened to her family."

I bristled. "I am her family."

"I'm sorry. Her ... family of origin? Whatever you call them, the texts don't mention any connection. So I can't tell if she knows who he is and she's covering her tracks, or if she just thinks she's running off to meet her boyfriend."

"Boyfriend ..." My mind reeled.

"If you read it without any context," Michelle continued, "it all looks pretty innocent. But knowing what we know, you can see him being patient. Planting seeds. Manipulating her to think that coming down here was her idea. Letting her think that she's in charge."

I slumped in my chair.

"The messages go back several months, and her whole trip down here is all there. She came down to meet him. She picked up work at the club while she waited for him, then the messages stop the day before we met you. He was careful. He got her right where he wanted her."

"My Vic would never ..." My words hung in the air. I couldn't even finish the sentence.

Tony leaned back, scratching the side of his face. "I don't want to alarm you."

"Too late for that, sir."

He shrugged. "Okay, that's fair. It's just, in my former line of work, I had occasion to, uh, 'take' a person or two." He curled his fingers around the word. I didn't think it'd be right to ask more questions, so I just nodded for him to continue.

"Sometimes it was a person who wanted us there. Who wanted away from where they were. But sometimes it was a person we needed. We were taking them from someplace they were comfortable to someplace where that was not in the cards."

My blood ran cold. "You kidnapped people?"

"Naw." He shook his head. "We captured a few high-value targets, but that's not the point. My point is that if you need someone to come with you, everything is easier if the person wants to come along."

"So you think they manipulated her?"

It was Kate's turn to shrug. "Maybe."

"They call it catfishing." Michelle's fingers paused over the keyboard as she explained. "It's a thing online. They pretend to be someone else and lure—"

"I know what catfishing is. I'm not that much older than you-all."

"So the question is whether they catfished her or whether she went knowing who this man was. Either way, I don't think they just snatched her up."

"But how do you know it's really this Mendoza guy? It could be anyone."

"He used his own phone. Not a burner."

"But then the Marshals? The FBI ...?"

Kate took my hand. "Cases like this are complicated. Are they watching Mendoza? Probably. But right now, your priorities and theirs are very different. Even if they are monitoring his every move, their prize is Sandoval, along with enough evidence to lock him away and dismantle his entire organization."

"And if finding your daughter would blow that operation—" Tony hesitated like he was waiting for me to fill in the blank. But I needed to hear him say it. So I waited.

He finally finished his thought. "You're gonna get nothing more than lip service from them. They'll tell you what you want to hear. They'll tell you they're looking for her. They'll tell you they've got your back. But you need to understand why that might not be true. You are Victoria's best chance to get out of this. Not the government. She's their chance to catch a big fish."

Michelle nodded. "Tony's right. It's not malicious. It's just a conflict of interests."

"But if they have her, why is Sandoval coming for me now?"

Kate grimaced. "Loose ends."

I looked over at the two men sitting on the stage. "What do they have to say?"

"Nothing." Tony's gaze was fixed on them as he answered. "I know how to get people to talk, but these guys are low-level door-kickers. They get their orders, they follow them, they get paid. The less they know, the better for Sandoval. And they clearly know less."

Kate's eyebrow ticked up. "Tony, he needs to know everything. Tell him."

"Well, okay. I did get one thing from them, but I'm not sure you need to know it."

I took a breath and squared my shoulders. "Young man, I'm stronger than I look. I might not be able to fight off a bunch of big, young thugs, but I certainly can handle the truth."

"Okay. I did get them to tell me their orders. They couldn't tell me why, of course, but they were supposed to pick you up and deliver you to a mercenary in West Palm. El Tigre."

I was confused. "Why would you think I couldn't handle that?"

He lifted his shirt to reveal a long scar along his side. "Because he gave me this right before I killed him back in '14."

18

SHAMELESS
CHRIS NILES

MY MIND WAS STILL SPINNING as Kate's rattletrap Civic bounced down the gravel lane leading through the center of Shark Key. With just a few exceptions, the campground was full, every wide site hosting anything from a tent to those massive diesel tour-bus rigs.

El Tigre.

I thought names like that were only found in bad thriller novels. But here we were. Apparently, some zombie tiger drug-lord wanted me, furniture salesman Harvey Thackerson of the South Boston Thackersons. Go figure.

Tony twisted in his seat. "When those guys miss their check-in, El Tigre will start getting antsy. We don't have a lot of time, but we have enough to teach you a few things that might keep you alive. But you're gonna have to pay attention."

"I may look like an old man, but I served back in the day. I know a thing or two."

"That's a good foundation. But things have changed since then, Harvey. Tactics. Weapons. We'll brush you up on the most critical skills." He turned to Kate as she slowly dodged potholes in the lane. "Chuck'll have everything ready?"

She nodded. "Whaler is loaded and fueled, and I bet he's firing up the outboard right now."

She guided the Civic through a break in a row of thick sea grapes and past a low, white, concrete shower-house, then the lane opened into a wide, crushed-coral parking lot. Sea grape hedges separated the lot from docks on both shorelines, and the restaurant with its wide deck occupied most of the northern tip of the island. To the right, the marina office and camp store sat in front of a long, low workshop. And a little, yellow, concrete-block house perched between them.

As Kate eased the car into a parking space, a scruffy man about ten years my junior appeared through a break in the hedge, twirling his finger in the air.

"She's running and loaded. Heard tell the FWC's been out on the flats this morning, so watch yourselves, okay? You don't want them asking questions with that much gear aboard."

Kate winked at him. "You're so sweet, worrying about us like that. We'll be okay, Chuck. I promise. You wanna come with?"

"Nah, Babette's got her hands full with the restaurant. Justin's not back yet and that guy with the straw hat who was helping out in the office disappeared last night in that O'Day ..." He trailed off as he peered into the backseat at me. "Wait, ain't that your boat?"

I shrugged. "Not anymore. He earned it. But I'll put money down you won't see him back here again."

I folded myself out of the Civic's backseat, cradling my tender elbow as I slammed the door shut behind me. "Don't happen to have any ibuprofen in that office, do you?"

Chuck answered with a single nod, then spun on his heel and sauntered back into the little office. As we walked past, he popped back out shaking a little plastic bottle.

"This oughta hold you a while."

I swallowed four of the capsules dry and followed Kate and Tony to a skiff sitting low in the water at the end of the dock, its motor chugging on the transom. They helped me aboard, and Kate directed me to a bench seat in the bow. Tony lifted the seat of the bench oppo-

site me, nodded, then dropped it back into place. He threw off the
bow line, then gently shoved off before he dropped onto the seat,
propping his feet on the seat beside me.

Kate threw off the stern line, then returned to the center console
and nudged the throttle forward. The outboard grumbled, and the
boat slipped away into the clear turquoise water.

I leaned over the rail and watched the sandy bottom below us
until we eased out of the no-wake zone, then Kate pushed the throttle
forward and the boat climbed up and skimmed along the surface,
racing toward a cut between two islands on the horizon.

She guided the little boat across the water, gently easing it
through unmarked cuts and avoiding the shallow spots that were
pocked with the telltale streaks where unsuspecting tourists had run
their rental boats aground. Tony pointed out a few of the deeper
gouges as we sped past, and I thanked Neptune that I'd managed to
guide the O'Day through the shallow waters without scraping her
bottom.

Before long, Kate piloted the skiff through the cut between the
islands, then took a wide turn to port and pointed her at a brilliant
blue cove tucked into a horseshoe-shaped island.

She eased back on the throttle, and the little boat settled down
with the waterline hitting just inches below her gunwales.

"She's sitting a little low, isn't she? What's loaded in those fish
boxes?"

Tony just grinned as Kate eased the bow up to a tangle of
mangrove roots at the far point of the horseshoe. He tossed a line
ashore, then hopped to his feet and leaped onto the tangle, landing as
sure-footed as a mountain goat. He made quick work of tying the
boat, then he pulled the bow close and grabbed it by the rail.

"Harvey, you can climb across, and if you can find a good grip, it'd
be a big help if you could hold her here while we unload?"

As I crouched at the bow and carefully found a foothold on the
tangled roots, Kate began flipping storage lockers open. She pulled
case after case out, lining them up along the bow. I counted five as
she passed them to Tony, and he set each one on the sand beyond the

tree line. Finally, Kate herself climbed onto the island and nodded to me. I released the little boat and she drifted back on the current, pulling the line tight and settling in.

"This one's the lightest," Tony said, handing me a long, flat case.

I reached for it with my good arm and fell in line between the two of them as they made their way down a narrow path. As the vegetation thickened, the path forked, and Kate led us off to the right into the deeper thicket until it opened up around a murky brown lagoon.

Kate nodded to a fallen tree about halfway up the shore to the right. "A few years ago, I followed a treasure map and found a fishing trophy belonging to Ernest Hemingway on that shore right over there."

Tony leaned over my shoulder. "I won't mention the crocodile or the thug she had to fight off for it ... Chuck's shoulder still hasn't quite recovered from that one."

I looked the little blonde up and down. In the daylight, out here in the wilderness, she didn't look like the type of person I'd expect to fight her way out of a paper bag. But she moved with confidence, and if a Navy SEAL was willing to let her take charge, then I figured that was good enough for me. The two of them clearly had a connection.

"You two look like you've done this before?"

Tony shrugged as he assembled a canvas folding table. Kate pulled a smile that didn't quite reach her eyes.

"A time or two. The Lower Keys are paradise for a lot of people, but trouble still has its little nooks and crannies to lurk around in. And when trouble decides it's time to come out and play, it's up to folks like us to shut down the game." She grabbed a stapler and a stack of paper targets sporting photos of various vermin, then jogged across and began tacking them to trees across the lagoon.

I turned to Tony, who was opening pelican cases to reveal a veritable arsenal nestled in black foam.

"Whoa."

Tony grinned. "We won't need all of these. I just wanted to see what felt the best in your hands. Let's start here."

He lifted a thin gun with a long, narrow barrel, slapped a magazine in, and held it out to me. It had been almost forty years since I'd held a pistol, but some habits were drilled in deep enough that my hands remembered what to do even if my brain didn't. My fingers found the release, dropping the mag into my left hand. I quickly counted ten tiny rounds, slid it back into the grip, and racked one into the chamber.

"Twenty-two. Light and accurate."

"It might not stop a raging bull, but it's great for target practice. Let's see what you've got."

Kate strolled back across our line, and Tony pointed at one of the targets about twenty yards away.

I lifted the gun with both hands. My elbow screamed, and my arm instinctively dropped and curled around my belly. I didn't want Tony and Kate to see me as a useless old man, though, so I adjusted my stance, stretched my right arm out, and lined up on the target.

POP POP POP POP POP

I unloaded five rounds, one right after the other, then stopped to see how I'd done. As I squinted at the paper looking for holes I couldn't find, Kate's gentle laugh told me what my eyes couldn't see. I hadn't hit even one.

"Here, let's try this." Her soft fingers probed at my bad elbow, massaging it as she guided the arm up and straight. "You're not gonna be much help if we can't get this arm working for you. And I know you really want to be helpful."

I lifted the gun back up, and with her supporting my elbow, I tested out a two-handed grip. This time, it felt a little better. The combination of her massage and the ibuprofen were working.

"Now," her soft voice was practically singing in my ear, "real gentle, with your right hand—you're right-handed?"

I nodded.

"Okay, with your right hand, push toward the target, like you're reaching for it."

I stretched toward it and slipped my finger onto the trigger.

"Wait." Tony strode toward us and pulled the gun from my hand.

"We didn't cover the Big Rules. One: Never point the barrel at anything you're not willing to hit, even if you think it's empty."

"Two," Kate continued, "never, ever touch your finger to the trigger until you're ready to pull it. Here." She took the gun from Tony, pointed it toward the trees, and gripped it with her index finger extended flat along the trigger guard. "Always like this, until you're ready to fire. Always."

I nodded as Kate extended the weapon to me, grip first, its barrel directed toward the ground downrange. I guess my habits were rustier than I thought. I stretched my finger parallel to the barrel and lifted it toward the target with both hands, ignoring the pain shooting down my elbow.

Kate rubbed around the knot. "How's that doing? Is it gonna hold for you?"

"It's not happy, but it'll do, I think."

"Okay, so now push toward the target with your right hand, and then pull back with your left. Push, pull. See how that feels more stable?"

Damned if she wasn't right. As I increased the pressure with my left hand, the gun stopped shaking and it became easy to line the sights up on the center of the target.

"Now, slow and steady. Keep your eye on the sights and the sights lined up. Just one shot for now. And don't jerk the trigger, just gently squeeze it. Let it surprise—"

A single shot popped from the gun's barrel, and it did, in fact, surprise all three of us. Especially the fact that it hit just an inch off the center of the target.

"See," Tony pointed to the brand new, bright yellow hole. "Slow is smooth, and smooth is fast. Take your time and finish that magazine."

"These color-changing targets make it really easy to see your results, especially at distance. Plus they're fun." Kate stepped back, and one at a time, I put three more yellow holes in the body of the target, and one gray one just outside the outline.

Kate practically sang as she took the .22 from me, snapped a fresh magazine in, and popped ten rounds into the center mass of a zombie groundhog.

Over the next couple of hours, the sun rose above the tree line and pounded down on the murky surface of the lagoon, and Tony and Kate worked me up through the various guns they'd brought, from handguns and rifles to a seven-round shotgun that practically knocked Kate off her feet when she fired it.

And as the sun eased its way west, we moved over to the shade and cleaned and packed everything back in the pelican cases. Kate asked me to go collect the targets, and I stacked them all up neatly, the bears and rabbits and raccoons and groundhogs all peppered with holes. I presented them to her as an offering of thanks.

With these two on my side, I was beginning to think we had a chance to get my Victoria back.

19

SHAMELESS
CHRIS NILES

THE AFTERNOON SUN was pounding down as Kate eased the little skiff up to the dock. Kara was standing there holding up one of the thugs by his collar. As Tony tossed one dock line around a cleat and hopped up, Kara greeted us, "*Mi hermano's* got something to tell you about."

"C'mon, they gonna kill me."

The corner of Kara's lip ticked up. "You already told me, so they're gonna kill you either way. It'll be more helpful if you tell him directly, though. And if you're helpful, maybe we'll be inclined to be helpful back."

The three of us followed Kara as she dragged the guy across the dock and up a short flight of stairs to the deck that wrapped all the way around the north point of the island. It was dotted with tables covered by wide umbrellas. Kara shoved the guy into a chair and hovered behind him. Kate and I settled into the shade opposite him, while Tony strolled over to the bar and brought back a bucket of bottled water on ice.

He cracked the tops of two bottles and handed them to me and Kate. Then he looked at the thug and nodded to me.

My pulse quickened. I don't know how to interrogate someone. I didn't even know where to start. My mind raced, and I took a sip of water to buy a minute to put my thoughts in order. Just as I was forming the first question, the guy started running his mouth.

"We're not here for the girl. We didn't take the girl, I swear. You got it all wrong, man. We're just here to stop you looking for her."

I froze, the water bottle just an inch from my mouth. "You what?"

"Two nights ago, I get a call there's a job in the Keys. Guy asking around about his missing daughter needs to stop asking around. I meet the client at a hotel bar in West Palm. Marina behind it. So I'm sitting out there watching the boats, and I see two guys and a really pretty girl on the dock behind this big fancy yacht. You know, the kind guys like me only get to work on. Anyway, biggest guy of the three glances up then turns back to the other dude and points to shore. Then he takes the girl's elbow, and she got this big tattoo. Same as in the pictures the skinny Black woman showed me. Brightest flowers I ever seen ..."

He kept talking, but my mind stopped processing any of his words. It took me straight back to our front porch. Victoria was twelve. It was a Sunday afternoon in August. Hot as all hell. Martha and I were drinking iced tea, and the kids from the block were playing street hockey. Vic was tending goal. She dove to block a shot, and her bare arm landed on the pavement and slid far enough to scrape the hell out of her and burn what was left.

I was down the steps and halfway across the lawn before her scream even started. But in the couple of seconds it took me to get to her, she was bleeding everywhere and her whole arm looked like ground beef. I scooped her up, threw her in the car. Raced to the ER. They cleaned it all out and bandaged her up and filled her with antibiotics, and she spent the rest of the month in the air condition-ing. It finally healed up, but she had a scar on her arm that never faded. And the more time she spent outside, the more pale it looked against her tanned skin, and the more self-conscious she got. She kept begging us to let her get a tattoo to cover it, but one look at the faded green mistakes on my body got her a quick no from Martha. Me, too. I didn't want my beautiful baby girl ruining her body. Better to let God heal it up, I told her. But Vic was pulling away from us in so many ways. The more I begged her, the more determined she was to do it.

Day she turned eighteen, she was down at the tattoo parlor getting that damned flower pattern outlined. Took him four sessions, but in the end, I had to admit he did a good job. Lines were sharp. Colors were bright. Damn sight better than the drunken dockside fools I'd used, anyway.

So maybe I was wrong. It happens every now and then.

And as the fool in front of me spilled words onto the table that I didn't hear, my memory traced every line of every flower on my baby girl's arm. I could imagine that gorilla taking her by the elbow and pushing her onto the boat. Beyond that, I forced my imagination to stop. She'd been with them for two nights, and I wasn't going to allow them to keep her for a third.

I pushed my chair back, guzzled down the rest of my water, and leveled my stare at Kate. "I'm gonna need a ride to West Palm Beach."

She smiled. "You're gonna need a lot more than that, Harvey. But we've got your back." She turned to Tony. "Let's load up."

20

SHAMELESS
CHRIS NILES

FOUR HOURS LATER, after an interminably long ride in stop-and-go traffic all the way through the Keys, I followed Tony and Kate through the lobby of an older hotel that looked straight out of the 1930s, Whiskey on a loose lead at Kate's heel. As they passed the bar, Tony leaned across, slipped a bill to a tall, light-haired bartender and spoke quietly in his ear. The man slid the money into his pocket with a nod, and in the blink of an eye, we were passing outside and across the lawn to the docks.

"What did you say to him?"

"Not important. Only thing you need to know is that none of us were ever here. Got that?"

I glanced around. We certainly were here, and I was determined to stay until I had my girl in my arms again.

Tony nudged Kate and ticked his head toward the biggest yacht on the dock. Then he stopped, grabbed her hand, and pulled her into an embrace that for all the world looked like he was saying goodbye. I nearly tripped over Whiskey, then stumbled back a couple of steps.

Tony kissed Kate on the forehead, then clung to her hand as she walked on, only releasing her hand when he couldn't reach it anymore.

Then he spun back to me, all business, and adjusted the heavy backpack dangling from his shoulder. "Follow me."

He walked so fast I could barely keep up, heading toward the parking lot, then doubling back along a line of palm trees and taking a spot behind a small, concrete-block storage building along the dock. I finally caught up and settled in behind him, my breath coming in gasps for the next couple of minutes. I wiped my sweaty face with the tail of the shirt I'd been wearing for two days, and with a gasp realized I'd left all my clothes and the very few possessions I had on the boat with Troy Bodean. Once I got Vic back, we'd need to take a hell of a trip to the mall.

I was pulled from my reverie by a not-so-gentle elbow to my middle. Tony was pointing to the dock near the stern of the big yacht. Kate stood on the dock with Whiskey sitting beside her, his head slightly tilted and his tongue hanging loose out his open mouth. Two burly men in black tactical pants and tight T-shirts stood on the deck above. Kate's body language looked loose and flirty—a far cry from the tight and focused woman with the even tighter, more focused dog we'd walked away from a moment before.

She kept running her hand through her hair, and her curls shook as she bounced on the balls of her feet.

We inched forward. Tony dropped to one knee and lowered his pack as Kate's voice echoed across the cove's glassy water.

"... heard there'd be some fun here? Some"—her head tilted to the side—"action? My friends said to look for the girl with the flowered tattoo on the really big boat."

The two men stiffened. There's no way she didn't notice, but you wouldn't know it the way she talked. "This is the biggest boat, so I figured I'd start here. Maybe I'm a little early, but I thought maybe I'd catch the worm? You know, the early bird and all that?" She kind of stomped her foot like a woman much younger than her age might do. "Come on, guys. I know somebody in there can hook me up."

I could feel every muscle in Tony's body vibrating beside me. He reached into the bag, his stare still fixed on Kate. Without looking, he pulled a short rifle from the backpack, unfolded the stock, then snapped a magazine into place.

"Don't touch the trigger unless we're both down. Do you understand me?"

I nodded, then realized he still hadn't taken his eyes off the boat.

"Yeah. I am the last resort. Got it." I took the weapon and eased myself down to the ground beside him.

He finally glanced around at me. "Settle in, keep yourself loose, but stay ready. If everything falls apart, you'll need to shoot fast and keep the concrete between you and the boat. If it gets loud, help won't take long to show up." His eyes flicked back up toward the bar, then he pulled an empty can out of his pack and hopped to his feet. With a final nod, he sauntered around the building and across the thick Bermuda grass.

Dressed in loose khaki pants, a white long-sleeved shirt, tattered ball cap, and flip-flops, Tony looked like every South Florida beach bum I'd ever imagined. He carried the beer can like it wasn't his first of the day. But I'd watched him tuck a handgun the size of a small dog into his waistband and strap another smaller one around his ankle. And he hadn't sent Kate in there unarmed, either.

I could tell these two could handle themselves even without Whiskey, but that boat was big, and there were sure to be more armed men than I could see. So I arranged myself against the sturdy building, the gun's stock against my shoulder and my finger flat along the guard, just like Kate showed me. I'd only known these people for a few hours, but they were already family.

Tony stumbled up the dock.

"Ahoy! G'd afternoon!" He raised his beer can and waggled it in the air, then rolled his head toward Kate. "Nice dog you got there, hot stuff. Lookin' for a party? I can—"

"I'm okay, thanks. These guys are gonna take good care of me." She turned back toward the men in black. "Aren't you, big guys?"

The two men traded a glance. The second they took their eyes off Kate, Whiskey leaped over the gunwale and latched his powerful jaws onto the bigger man's arm. The second man lunged at the dog, but

Kate was over the rail right behind him and wrapped herself over his back, her elbow expertly crooked around his throat. The smaller man stumbled back and slammed Kate into the bulkhead, but she clung to him like a monkey. He staggered around toward the stern rail and dropped as Whiskey dragged the big man to the deck beside him.

Kate bounced to her feet and lined her sights up on the two.

"Whiskey, release."

The dog raced to Kate's side and stood at attention. Then a dark-skinned man in a white embroidered shirt and sharply pressed khakis stepped out from the shaded salon, pistol pointed at Kate. Whiskey spun, then froze.

"Drop it." Tony's command rang out across the water, and the man's gaze shot down to the dock where Tony held his .45 steady. The man stretched his arms apart, and as his gun dropped to dangle from his finger, another shadow appeared on the deck. My breath caught in my throat.

Victoria.

I dropped the rifle to the grass and began to push to my feet, filled with joy. Then she shouted.

"Don't shoot!" She ran forward and positioned herself between Tony and the third man, wrapping her arms around him protectively. "Whatever you want, you can have, just don't hurt us."

I launched myself across the lawn. "Victoria, honey! Over here. These people are with me. I've come to take you home, baby girl. You're safe now."

The words kept spilling out of my mouth as I ran as fast as I could manage toward the dock. Victoria and the man began inching back toward the salon.

"Vic, I'm here. You're okay."

Then her voice rang out across the marina as an army of huge armed men swarmed across the deck and onto the dock, quickly overtaking Kate, Whiskey, and Tony. Victoria straightened to her full height and turned toward me.

"Of course I'm okay, Harvey. Why wouldn't I be? This is my boat."

PART III

DOUGLASS PRATT

Douglas Pratt is the author of the Chase Gordon Tropical Thriller Series and the Max Sawyer Mystery Series. When he's not writing, he tries to spend his spare time on his sailboat.
You can learn more about Douglas at www.douglas-pratt.com where you can sign up for his newsletter and grab a free story.

21

SHAMELESS
DOUGLAS PRATT

EVERYTHING HAPPENED SO FAST. The marina spun around me, and my knees seemed to buckle.

Her boat?

"This is a waste of time!" the man in the white shirt shouted. I looked at him. He was in his late thirties.

The guy ordered, "Bring the old man. We are leaving. Romano, when we are gone, take the rest away."

I saw Vic glance back at the man. There was something in her eyes. "Rico, leave them," she said. "It'll draw too much attention."

Rico glanced at Vic and then at Romano, the one who held a gun on Tony. Rico gave a curt nod. Whatever it meant moved Vic's attention to the dock. She glanced at Kate and Tony, shaking her head.

"Come on, *mi amor*," Rico Mendoza called to my daughter. My skin crawled to think about this vile man anywhere near her.

"No, Vic!" I rushed toward her, wishing I hadn't tossed my rifle aside. Two men blocked me, grabbing my arms.

"Harvey, stop," Victoria ordered. "Don't do this."

"You don't understand." How could I explain everything? How could I tell her that the man she was with worked for the people who had killed her parents? Did he know who she was? I was so confused.

"Leave him," Vic said.

Rico Mendoza lifted both hands, questioning her. "But you wanted him to leave you alone," Mendoza said.

She sent an icy stare at me before she turned back to Mendoza. "He knows now." With a last glance over her shoulder at me, she added, "He knows I don't want to go back."

"Victoria," I pleaded.

The two men on either side of me tightened their grip.

"What are you going to do with us?" Kate shouted at them.

Mendoza ignored her as he put his palm on the small of Victoria's back.

Bile rose in my throat as tears welled in my eyes. I let out a bellowing howl of rage, and despite a bad back and aged joints, anger and adrenaline fueled me. My arms flailed, and the man on my right lost his grip for a second. It was enough leverage to drive my right fist into the face of the one on my left.

For a split second, I was fifty years younger. Then my hand struck the man's face. Whether I did much damage to him, I wasn't sure, but my fingers throbbed as if I just dropped a recliner on them.

I saw the fist as it slammed into my face. The second blow was harder, and it landed on the back of my head.

"No!" I heard Kate yell as my knees buckled, sending me to the wooden dock.

Before I could get up, I heard the engines of the yacht roar as the vessel pulled off the dock. I rolled onto my back as three gunshots echoed off the water.

The man I'd hit in the face fell on top of me, and I pushed his lifeless body off me. When I was out from under him, I saw two men moving down the steps from the direction of the hotel. Both men held what looked like 45-caliber pistols. Tony was pointing a gun at the one Mendoza had called Romano.

"Everyone good?" one of the new men shouted. It took a second to recognize him as the bartender who Tony had whispered to. Now, he didn't resemble any bartender I'd ever seen. He moved with the other man like they were in sync. Both men had matching tattoos peeking out from under their right sleeves. I could see the image of a skull and an oar poking out.

What the hell was going on? My head throbbed from the blow I took. My fingers reached around to feel a sticky mess in my hair. There was a decent-sized gash oozing blood.

The bartender caught me by the arm. "You okay?" he asked as he pulled me to my feet.

"I'm glad I saw you," Tony said.

"The Corps is always happy to save a Squid's ass," the bartender quipped back.

"What's going on?" I asked. "Where's Victoria? Kate!" I saw Kate sprawled on the deck, trying to get up. She had a bigger cut on her head than I did. "Are you alright?"

"Dizzy," she said. "Tony?"

"We need to get you to the hospital." Tony took a look at her head. "That's gonna need some stitches."

Kate waved it off for a second before she swooned a little, catching Tony's arm. "Okay, I guess I need a few minutes."

Still holding a gun on Romano, Tony glanced at the bartender and the other man. "Guys, I hate to do this to you, but I think Kate's out of this one for a bit."

"I can get an ambulance," the other man offered, training his gun on Mendoza's man.

Kate shook her head slowly. "No, Tony can get me there. This is a big enough mess."

Tony glanced at the two men. "Gordon, this is Harvey. He's going to need a little help, too."

"Go on," the bartender, who I guessed was Gordon, told him. "Jay can clear this all up."

The other man turned to look at Gordon. "Three dead bodies. And you want me to clear it up?"

Gordon shrugged. "We still have this one." He pointed at Romano. "Why don't we blame the whole thing on him?"

Romano turned his head, looking at the bodies of his comrades. He shuddered.

"I'm sorry," I said to the bartender. "Who are you?"

"Sorry, Harvey," the bartender replied. "I'm Chase Gordon. This here's Jay Delp."

"You guys mind if I get her out of here?" Tony asked.

Delp nodded to Tony.

Holding onto Tony for balance, Kate called, "Harvey, we'll be back to help."

"Kate, you've done enough," I promised. "Thank you."

"I'm sorry," she said as she limped away.

Whiskey followed the two humans as they climbed the steps that Gordon and Delp had descended a few minutes earlier.

"Who are you guys again?" I asked.

"Tony recognized me in the bar," he said. "We crossed paths back in Afghanistan once. I guess he thought he might need some backup."

"That's what he was whispering to you?"

Gordon nodded. "He basically asked me to keep an eye out in case things got out of hand."

"That man on the boat?" Delp asked in a thick Southern accent I couldn't place. "Do you know who that was?"

I nodded. "Yeah, Rico Mendoza."

"That's who I thought," Delp confirmed. "I have to call this in, Flash."

Gordon shrugged and pointed at Romano, who was still standing with his hands in the air. "This one might want to consider becoming a state's witness."

Romano shook his head. "*No habla ingles.*"

Gordon chuckled. "Yeah, you understand just fine, don't you?"

Delp stepped away and pulled a phone from his pocket.

"Who's he calling?" I asked.

"He's a cop," Gordon explained. "He feels obligated to report this kind of thing."

"Oh." If the police were involved, it wouldn't take long for the U.S. Marshals to get involved. How much danger would that put Victoria in? If she was lucky, Mendoza had no idea who she really was. Plus, what would Cunningham do if he found out she was involved with them? There were some rules about returning to one's old life that could nullify the protection.

"Listen, Mr. Gordon, there's a problem," I tried to explain.

"Harvey, please call me Chase. I'd say Mr. Gordon was my father, but I prefer not to remember him."

I remembered Troy Bodean saying something like that a day ago ... wait, was it only a day? Maybe it was more. Everything was running together so quickly. I shook the thought away.

"Do the police really need to get involved?" I asked.

Chase turned toward each of the bodies. "This isn't exactly shoplifting," he pointed out. "Otherwise I'd agree with you. Dealing with the headache is a bit much, but my boss doesn't care for dead bodies decorating her docks. She seems to think it's bad for business."

"That was my daughter," I said.

"The girl on the boat?"

I nodded curtly.

"What does this Mendoza have to do with her?"

"It's a complicated story, Chase." I was afraid to talk too much in front of Romano.

"What's your name?" Chase asked the man in front of him. The cartel thug remained stoic.

"I heard Mendoza call him Romano," I told Chase.

"Romano." Chase rolled the name around in his mouth. "Like a nice *tomahto.*"

"Or a cheese," I added for no real reason.

Chase smiled at me. "No, more like a tomato. They're much easier to squash."

I watched Romano swallow. So did Chase.

"I saw that, Romano," he noted. "He said he doesn't speak English, but he knew what 'squash' meant."

Romano blinked.

"Harvey, do you see that sign over there?" Chase asked, pointing the barrel of his 45 toward a placard on the wall.

"The 'No Swimming' one?" I asked.

"Yeah, do you know why they don't want you to swim around a marina?" he asked.

I didn't have an answer, which made me feel stupid, since I'd just driven a boat all the way down from Boston. Was this some common knowledge I should have been privy to?

"In order to power all these boats, there's a lot of electricity running along the dock," Chase explained. "Only thing is—unlike running power through the ground or in overhead lines—this is salt water. Highly conductive. While you can swim around out in the middle of Lake Worth over there and have no problems, when you get close to the slips there's juice buzzing through the water all around. It just needs the closest path to ground out."

Romano looked down at the water.

"I didn't know that," I said. "Why don't the fish get electrocuted?"

"Same reasons that birds can sit on the electric wires, I guess," he answered.

Chase prodded Romano with the barrel. "Now, you have a choice, Romano. Learn English very quickly and answer some questions, or you can go for a swim. We can see how much juice is in the water."

Romano clenched his jaw.

"Where's Mendoza going?" Chase asked.

The henchman didn't respond.

"One more time," Chase said. "Where is Mendoza going? If you don't answer, you'll get wet."

Romano began shaking his head. "No, no, no," he said.

Chase lowered the gun and shook his head. With fear in his eyes, Romano twisted as if to run. Chase's palm caught Romano in on the shoulder, shoving him toward the water.

"No!" the man blurted out as he tumbled over the edge. The splash alerted Delp, who jogged toward us.

"Mendoza," Chase repeated, leaning over the water. "Do you feel the tingle yet? Sometimes it takes being in the right place, so I wouldn't move much."

"Get me out!" Romano screamed.

Chase twisted his head, flashing me a wry grin. "What do you know? I must be a good English teacher."

"What the hell?" Delp asked as he stopped beside Chase.

"He tried to run," Chase said.

"Sure he did," the detective responded in a heavy drawl.

"Get me out, please!" Romano said.

"Where's Mendoza going?" Chase asked again.

"South," Romano said as he thrashed about, trying to stay away from the dock. His eyes moved around as if he was judging how far he was from the pier.

"South is a big area," I pointed out, trying to follow Chase's play.

"They'll be in Biscayne Bay for a day or so before heading on to the Keys." Romano gasped as he struggled. The thug wasn't much of a swimmer, and he was tiring.

"You have any more details than that?" Chase asked.

Romano shook his head violently.

"Guess that will do," the bartender said. "Come over here and get out."

"The electric?" Romano, looking scared, pushed away from the side.

"How is he going to get out, Chase?" I wondered the same thing as Romano.

"I might have exaggerated," Chase said.

"What?" I asked.

"I mean, sure, there's a slight risk of electrocution in the water around the docks. That's why the sign is there, but it's pretty rare. The pier would need to be in disrepair for bare wires to be in the water. The Tilly is in tiptop shape, so it was a stretch."

"Good grief, Flash," Delp muttered as he bent over to pull Romano out of the water.

"Bastard." Mendoza's man spat as he rolled onto the deck, a puddle of water forming underneath him.

Chase shrugged off the insult as the man pushed to his feet. Romano's eyes burned with rage at being tricked by Chase.

I saw Romano's head snap back a millisecond before I heard the crack.

"Gun!" Jay Delp dropped to a crouch.

The wind rushed out of me as Chase tackled me. The two of us rolled off the dock into the water as another shot struck the wooden pier.

My head popped out of the water and I gasped for air.

"Stay down," Chase ordered, motioning to me. He raised the 45. Delp surfaced next to him.

"Anyone hit?" he asked us.

"No," Chase said. "Where are they?"

"That's a sniper," the deputy said. "They were aiming for Harvey."

"They shot Romano first," I said.

"But the second shot would have hit you," Delp said. "If Chase hadn't pulled you over, you'd be dead."

My stomach tightened. Was Victoria behind this? I didn't believe it. This was my little girl. She'd never try to kill me.

Of course, before today, I never would have believed she'd be in a relationship with a man like Mendoza. She just followed him onto that yacht like—I don't know—a mindless drone.

"Think they're gone?" Chase asked Delp.

Somewhere over the water, I heard the sounds of sirens growing closer.

"They won't stick around long," he admitted. "At least I wouldn't."

"I don't understand," I said.

Chase's voice was soothing. "Harvey, I get it. Right now, things are nuts. The only job you have is to breathe. In and out, okay?"

I obeyed him, sucking in slowly, then letting the air release. After several breaths, I calmed down a bit.

"Lift me up," Delp said to Chase.

Chase grabbed a slimy, barnacle-covered board with his left arm. His right extended to provide Delp a foothold. With a slight grunt, the bartender pulled and pushed the other man up until he rolled onto the dock.

"We got backup," he told us as two uniformed officers appeared. "I'm Detective Delp. Palm County."

"What's going on?" an officer asked.

"We have a sniper somewhere."

One officer talked into his radio as the other extended his hand down to me.

"Okay, Harvey," Chase said. "Your turn."

My knee pinged as I bent to press against Chase's hand. He shoved me up. Delp and the other officer caught my arms, pulling me onto the pier.

The surrounding scene could have been from an action movie. Four dead bodies sprawled across the dock.

"I have men arriving," the first officer, whose name tag read Claude, said to Delp. "They'll start canvassing the other buildings."

"Start with that garage," Delp said, pointing toward a building towering about a block to the west.

Chase stared at me for a second, curious. "Jay, you mind if I get Harvey here some dry clothes and take him up to the Manta?"

Detective Delp nodded. "Flash, if you have an extra shirt, I could use it." He pulled his wet polo shirt away from his skin.

"C'mon, Harvey." He set off down the dock, then stooped over and picked up a 9mm that one of the dead men had dropped. Discreetly, he handed it to me. "In case you need it," he whispered.

"Uh, Chase," I asked. "Where are we going?"

"Oh, sorry. I live over here."

I followed him down one of the walkways to a light tan sailboat. She looked to be a forty-footer. I didn't recognize the make, but I'd only been a sailor for a short time. "You live here?" I asked.

"This is *Carina*," he said as if he was introducing me to the boat.

"She's a beauty. What is she?"

"Tartan 40. She's not the biggest on the water, but she'll take me just about anywhere I want to go."

"Do you take it to the islands much?" I asked.

"As much as I can. Once I got out of the Corps, I wanted the freedom to go wherever I wanted. I'd spent a lot of years going places because the brass want me too. Now, I can pick up and head out at my own whim. Assuming my cruising kitty is filled enough."

"I just finished sailing an O'Day down from Boston."

"I bet that was quite a ride." He grinned.

For a moment, I thought about it. The journey wasn't something I enjoyed. It should have been. I'd never taken on such a feat, but the truth was that with every mile I covered, I worried about Vic and missed Martha. "It was my late wife's boat," I said.

Chase answered with a quick nod. There wasn't much else to say, I guess.

"Come aboard," he said. "I think I can at least find you a dry shirt."

I followed him as he stepped into the cockpit. Since I'd just come out of the water, I wasn't concerned with tracking mud aboard. Instead, I dripped oily harbor water onto his deck.

"How far have you cruised her?" I asked, stepping into the cockpit.

"I've taken her down through the Caribbean and almost all the way to Belize." Chase opened the companionway and climbed below deck. By the time I followed him down the steps, he was digging around in his hanging locker. He pulled out a short-sleeve, button-down fishing shirt, which he tossed to me. "I think there are some shorts in here, too. What size waist are you?"

There wasn't much chance I could squeeze into any waist size he wore. So I waved off the suggestion. "The shirt will be enough. I'm running out of clothes pretty fast."

Like most former military, Chase had no qualms about stripping down and changing in front of anyone. I think it came from years of living in cramped quarters. I know even way back when I served, there wasn't a chance my superior officers cared who I had to change in front of. I followed suit, pulling the wet shirt off and exchanging it for the dry one he offered me.

Once he had changed, he motioned for me to follow him. With another shirt in his hand, he climbed back on deck and off the boat.

"I don't know about you, Harvey," he said, "but I could use a drink."

"I'm from Boston. We have the blood of the Irish in us."

"Is it blood or whiskey?" He smiled.

"One and the same."

He led me back past the crowd of cops, where he tossed the extra shirt to Delp and told him we'd be in the bar.

"I think you have a story to tell." Chase looked at me as we sat down at the expansive mahogany bar.

"What's all the excitement, Chase?" another bartender, somewhere south of thirty, asked as he approached us.

"Attempted kidnapping, Hunter. Probably some human trafficking thing."

The way he said it made it feel blasé. As if it was a regular occurrence around here.

"What can I get you guys?" the kid asked.

"Rum punch," Chase told him.

"I'll take a Sam Adams if you have one," I said.

"Sam Adams. That's what I'd order in *Bahstan*." Chase exaggerated the accent.

"I like it." The kid set our drinks in front of us.

"Then drink up. Now about this story."

I genuinely liked Chase, but I didn't really know him. Of course, he'd saved my life twice within just a few minutes. And Tony seemed to trust him.

The thought of Tony made me wonder how Kate was doing. She seemed pretty tough, so I wasn't worried.

Did I trust Chase? My gut told me to. He had just killed a couple of Mendoza's men. That seemed like someone who wasn't in bed with the cartel.

"Okay," I said, "but it's dicey. The girl who followed Mendoza is my daughter."

"You told me that."

"Right, I'm sorry. Everything seems to be happening faster than my brain can process it."

Chase nodded. His blue eyes sympathized with me.

I continued, "She's adopted."

"By you?" he asked.

"Yes. My wife and I adopted her, but it wasn't a traditional adoption."

The bartender's eyebrow furrowed, and I realized he might be questioning the legitimacy of my claim. "No," I said. "It's nothing shady. Victoria was placed in our care by the U.S. Marshals. Her parents were murdered by the Sandoval Cartel."

His face switched from concern to surprise. "You're saying she was in witness protection to hide her from the people she's currently with?"

I nodded.

"Harvey, that's insane. Does she have any idea what she's doing?"

My head drooped as I shook it slowly.

"Here ya go, guys." Hunter set a second round on the bar in front of us.

"Thanks, Hunter," Chase said.

"I really don't know what she's thinking, Chase," I told him after taking another sip of the Sam Adams.

"Tell me everything."

I drained half the long neck before I started at the beginning. After I carried the tale to the encounter down at the Tilly Marina, he let out a sigh.

"This sounds fishy for sure." Chase took a sip of his drink. "It's like she wants to be with them."

I nodded, still confused by the whole thing. "Victoria's not perfect," I admitted. "I'm sure any kid who's adopted at that age has some transition issues. She watched her parents get killed. What does that do to a kid?"

"Harvey, everyone handles that kind of thing differently. It sounds like you and Martha offered her the best you could."

Emotion bubbled up inside me as tears slipped from my eyes. "I don't know how to protect my little girl."

Chase rested his hand on my shoulder. "She knows who killed her parents?"

"Yeah."

"Then it stands to reason that she's there for a reason."

"What reason?" I asked.

Chase shrugged. "If it were me, I'd be there to kill every last one of them."

"She wouldn't—"

"I don't know her." Chase twirled his glass around. "But that kind of darkness is easy to hide. Trust me."

"She'll never succeed."

He cocked his head. "I hope she has a good plan."

I started running every scenario through my head. If Victoria was on a suicide run, I needed to find her now. I realized I was grinding my teeth.

"He said they were going to Biscayne Bay or something like that?" I asked.

"Biscayne National Park."

"I need a car." I pushed away from the bar. Once my feet hit the floor, I said, "If I can get there before they leave, I can try to talk her into leaving with me."

Chase grabbed my arm. "Harvey, calm down for a second."

"Chase, you don't get it! I can't lose her too."

He nodded. "Of course not. But you can't just drive down to Biscayne. First, it's mostly a bay. A car won't get you very far."

"A boat, then?"

"Yeah, you can get there in a boat. Didn't you say you had an O'Day?"

"I kinda sold it," I said.

"Probably wouldn't do you much good." Chase laughed a little. "Even in *Carina*, it would take me a day to get down there. The yacht I saw your daughter on could be there in a few hours."

I slammed my fist on the bar in frustration. The handful of customers glanced my way. Chase raised his hand to wave off Hunter, signaling that everything was okay.

"I can probably get us a boat," he said. "But we'll need to know where to go."

I shook my head. "I'm not sure."

"Okay, let's burn that bridge when we get there. Let me handle the boat first."

His eyes shifted to the door leading out of the Manta Club into the lobby of the Tilly Inn. A dark-haired woman in her thirties stepped into the bar. She had an olive complexion and deep brown eyes I could see from across the room, in part because she was staring at us.

She motioned to Chase, who said, "Oh, I'll be right back."

As he followed the attractive woman out of the bar, Hunter came back by. "Need another Sam Adams?"

"Yeah, please."

"Were you part of whatever the cops are doing down at the marina?" he asked.

I glanced up at him. "Not really," I lied.

"I'm sure Chase was. Dude's like a total badass."

"Oh yeah?"

Hunter nodded. "Man, one time there was a small army that blew up the bar. Chase, like, fought them all off by himself. Even took out a hit man on his boat once."

"Sounds like a badass," I said.

Hunter leaned across the bar. "Let me just say—if I was in trouble, I'd be looking at Chase to save me."

Once the hero worship subsided, I asked, "Who was the woman?"

"Oh, Missy? She owns the hotel."

I nodded. "She's the boss, huh?"

"Yeah, but she's real cool. I like her."

Grinning, I said, "I can see why."

Hunter cackled. "Yeah, she's hot, too. Her husband's a dick, though, so there's that."

I shrugged because I didn't know what else to say. Hunter rounded the bar and returned with a fresh bottle of Sam Adams. As he turned to his other customers, I saw Chase and Missy come back through the door. They didn't touch, but there was an obvious intimacy between the two. It was none of my business, so I took a swallow of beer.

22

SHAMELESS
DOUGLAS PRATT

"Harvey, I think we might need to slip out before Jay comes back up here."

"Won't he be upset if we're gone?" I asked.

"Oh, yeah. But I'll tell him you were taking off after your daughter, and I couldn't let you go alone." He motioned for me to follow him, and I left my beer unfinished. I pulled a twenty-dollar bill from my wallet, tossing it on the bar. I hoped it covered our tab, but I doubted it. Chase didn't seem to care, and since he worked here, I guessed he would take care of it later.

He led me through the lobby. I studied the decor as we passed. The Tilly Inn seemed like it was from another time. The intricate marble columns and wainscoting seemed to belong in Italy, or maybe New York in the twenties.

"Where are we going?" I asked, tagging along close to Chase.

He stopped in the middle of the lobby. A tall, muscular Latino man in cowboy boots and a bright red shirt stood at the door. He looked mean, but maybe it was just because of the scar running along his cheek. On either side of him were two equally tough-looking men. The man with the scar pointed at Chase.

"Harvey, don't say anything to these guys. I'll do the talking. Whatever you do, don't tell them about your daughter."

"Who are they?" I asked.

"That's the head enforcer for the Andrade Cartel."

"Another one?"

"Don't worry about him," Chase assured me. "He won't cross us unless he has to."

"Has to? What does that mean?"

"It means I have to really piss him off first."

"Well, don't do that," I said.

Chase gave me a grin. "Don't worry, Harvey. Scar loves me."

"Scar?"

"Oh, don't call him that, though," he whispered as the enforcer stepped up to us.

"Gordon," the man said with a deep voice and Cuban accent.

"Esteban. Want to grab a table?" Chase waved his hand toward several marble-top round tables scattered around the lobby.

The man called Esteban or Scar cocked his head to the side quizzically. "There seems to be a heavy presence of *policía*."

"We had a problem," Chase told him.

"Let's take a ride." Esteban pointed toward the door.

"Come along, Harvey." Chase touched my arm. "I'm sure this ride will prove fruitful."

This setup made me nervous, but I followed Chase, even as fear quickened my pulse. Perhaps I had misjudged Chase. He might not work for the Sandoval Cartel, but he was certainly acquainted with this other one. Was he about to sell Victoria out? I wanted to protest but didn't know what might happen. I still had the 9mm Chase had given me. If he intended to turn on Victoria, I was ready to turn on him.

"Who is your friend, Gordon?" Esteban asked as he marched us through the revolving door to the street.

"Harvey, this is Esteban Velazquez," Chase introduced us. He didn't offer any other explanation.

"Hello." I fought to keep my voice steady.

The enforcer ignored my greeting. The Tilly Inn was located on Flagler Street. At this time of the evening, it was busy with worker bees getting off their jobs and heading home. Velazquez opened the door to a black Suburban sitting in the lot to the left of the entrance.

"Are you sure about this?" I asked Chase.

"It will be just fine," he said. I wasn't sure I could count on that. My fingers touched the gun in my pocket.

I climbed into the Suburban, which resembled the interior of a private jet more than an SUV. The seats had been rearranged so that they faced each other. A row of soft purple LED light strips ran along the ceiling. Chase slid into the seat next to me. Velazquez sat opposite us. The two men who had flanked him in the hotel lobby climbed into the front seat. The motor started, and the Suburban pulled out onto Flagler.

"What brings you around?" Chase asked.

"Trouble."

Chase was out of patience. "Let's cut the bull. We had a little incident with the Sandoval Cartel. How did you find out so fast?"

Velazquez stared at him, then his gaze shifted to me.

"What is up with the old man?" he asked.

"Old?" I balled my fists.

Velazquez shot me a glare. He leaned toward me and hissed, "Old."

"Doesn't matter," Chase said. "How did you get here so fast? It's at least an hour and a half in traffic from Miami. You had to leave before the shooting started."

"I was in the area," he said.

"Right." Chase raised an eyebrow. "Let's pretend that's true. Why are you here?"

"Rico Mendoza has something Señor Moreno wants. We would like it before it gets to Sandoval."

Chase cut his eyes over to me. "Something?"

"Someone," Velazquez replied with resignation.

They wanted Victoria. I didn't know why, but I'd be damned if I let this enforcer get his hands on her. The 9mm came out of my pocket. I thought I'd done it fast like Tony had shown me. Instead, Velazquez slammed me in the face with his fist before chopping the gun out of my hand.

"What is this, Gordon?" Scar leveled the 9mm at me.

"Whoa, Esteban, take it easy."

"You bastard." He'd split my lip but I forced the words out. "I won't let you have her."

Velazquez turned slowly to look at Chase. "What is he talking about?"

Chase sighed and looked at me. "I warned you to keep your mouth shut."

"They are looking for my daughter!" I shook with anger. "I'm not about to let you give them to her."

Velazquez chuckled. "This—what do you call it—Boy Scout, right? He doesn't give me anything. *Pero los dificultades.*"

"Esteban, you owe me." Chase shook his head.

The man stared at Chase.

"This isn't for Moreno or anyone. You owe me."

Velazquez nodded.

"His daughter is with Mendoza. She's in a lot of danger."

Estephan nodded again, and I swore there was some sympathy on his face.

"How long has she been with Mendoza?" he asked.

Chase looked at me. I answered, "I don't know, but they've been talking for a while."

"She might be trying to kill him. Trying to get to Sandoval."

Velazquez gave a little laugh. "How old is she?"

"Twenty-four," I told him.

The Cuban turned to Chase. "She sounds like she might be your blood."

He shook his head. "I don't think so."

"They will kill her," Velazquez said.

"Who is Julio looking for?" Chase asked. I wasn't sure who Julio was. This Moreno fellow they both talked about, I assumed.

The Suburban lurched as something crashed into the passenger's side. The SUV spiraled across the street, striking a couple of cars like a pinball.

"Get down!" Chase shouted, and instinct drove me to the floor of the vehicle.

Gunfire erupted, shattering the windows and peppering me with pebbles of tempered glass. Then the bullets stopped and footsteps approached on the passenger's side. Someone pressed a hand to my back, pushing me further down. I guessed it was Chase. The rear door opened, followed by six bangs that deafened me.

I rolled over with my ears still ringing to see Chase and Esteban Velazquez rising up, guns out. Velazquez fired my 9mm through the broken glass as Chase shot two men as they came through the rear door.

Hands covering my head, I tried to crawl under the seat to no avail. The gunfire slowed, and I felt more than saw Chase and Valazquez climb over me to exit the vehicle. Was it safe to raise my head? Another POP from outside the car.

"You good?" I heard Chase shout.

"Yeah," Velazquez responded. "The old man?"

"Harvey, you okay?"

"I ... uh, think so," I said, feeling around to make sure I wasn't bleeding. "What was that?"

"No time." Velazquez was curt. "We need to move. *¡Bájate, viejo!*"

"C'mon, Harvey." Chase grabbed my arm, pulling me free from the wreckage.

When I got my feet on to the pavement, I saw the carnage around us. The black Suburban was crushed on the rear end, but the bullet holes in the doors really added icing to the cake.

Velazquez peered into the front seat where his two men slumped forward, riddled with bullets.

"We need off the streets," he told Chase, who nodded.

Sirens sounded down the street, and Chase grabbed my arm, pulling me away from the scene, which was already crawling with gawkers.

"Damned cell phone cameras." Velazquez cursed as he cut between two buildings. "In here." He jerked a fire door open.

"Who was that?" Chase asked.

"El Tigre."

"Wait, what?" My already pounding heart accelerated. "El Tigre? The men in Key West were supposed to take me to him."

Velazquez stopped to look at me. "El Tigre wants you?"

I shrugged. "That's what the man said."

"Wait a second." Chase looked at me. "Who is this El Tigre?"

"I don't know," I said. "I thought he worked for Sandoval."

"El Tigre is not a man." Velazquez moved toward a flight of stairs.

"Like a ghost or something?" I asked.

He paused on the step, looking over his shoulder at me. "No—like a woman."

Chase looked confused. "Why would she use the name 'El Tigre' if she's a woman?"

"I'll let you ask her when you find her," the Cuban said.

"Who is she, then?"

"Only rumors." Velazquez shrugged. "Señor Moreno has said she is Sandoval's daughter."

"Why is she trying to kill me?" I asked.

"She has been attacking Sandoval for years. Now she had built a small army. As you can see, she has no problem killing anyone."

"Well, she didn't succeed," Chase said.

"Perhaps she didn't know what a pain in the ass it was to kill you, Gordon."

"I do try." The former Marine saluted.

"Wait." I reached a hand toward Velazquez. "Is she the one you are after?"

The Cuban stared at me.

"You said you wanted it before it 'gets to Sandoval.' It sounds like El Tigre wants to kill her father, but you want her first. Why?"

The man scowled at Chase, who said, "Don't look at me like that. Harvey's connected a few good dots."

Velazquez remained silent.

"Harvey, I can make some guesses," Chase said. "Moreno is one of the biggest drug dealers—"

Velazquez shot him a glare, and Chase reworded his sentence. "I mean to say, Moreno runs one of the biggest import businesses in Florida. Someone like Sandoval is competition, and like any businessman, it's all about leverage."

"How much leverage could he get with a daughter that's trying to kill the man?" I asked.

"It's a weird business." Chase took a breath. "Moreno might want to make her an asset, or he might want to trade her to Sandoval for a piece of his action. I doubt Esteban is at liberty to tell us much about their plan."

"None of that explains why she's after me." I rubbed my sore elbow. "And why does it affect Victoria?"

Chase turned to look at Esteban Velazquez. "Do you know?"

The enforcer shook his head. "I did not know this Victoria at all before you told me."

"She needs to stay out of your sights," I said.

Velazquez crossed his arms. "I gave Gordon my word."

I wasn't sure how much I could trust that, but my options were fairly limited at the moment.

"Perhaps El Tigre is after you to protect your daughter," Velazquez said.

"Protect Victoria? How would they even know each other?"

"It only appears as if they have the same agenda."

"Mendoza's man mentioned they were heading to Biscayne Bay," Chase said to Velazquez. "What could that be for?"

The man shrugged. "I can't say what Sandoval's business is. Biscayne is a good stopping-off point from the Bahamas. Or he could be meeting someone. The bay is big and open, offering a private place to meet. The rangers are too busy with the tourists to pay a lot of attention."

"You speak with experience," I said.

Valazquez smirked. "My experience is quite varied."

"The cops are going to be all over your Suburban," Chase said.

"We can't stay here too long."

"Agreed."

"Do you know any way we can find out where they are going?" Chase asked Velazquez.

"He can't call his daughter?" the man said, and I was about to lay into him when Chase motioned for me to wait.

"Let's not disparage anyone's daughter, big guy."

"We could always ask El Tigre," I said.

"Are you kidding?" Chase shook his head. "The woman tried to kill you."

"If she's working with Victoria, I just don't believe she intends to kill me," I said. "I can't believe Vic would do that."

"Harvey," he said, then paused.

Velazquez cut in. "This doesn't seem prudent."

"How deadly do you think this woman is?" I asked the drug enforcer.

He glanced between me and Chase. "Very."

"Exactly," I replied. "She's supposed to be good. Why else would they call her 'The Tiger'? But she's managed to miss me twice."

"Barely."

"Come on, Chase. On the dock, did she have time to shoot me after she hit Romano?"

Chase considered it, tilting his head side to side as he realized the answer. "I suppose she did."

"What if she drove us into the water to buy some time?"

"And the attack on my car?"

"Maybe that was all on you?" I suggested. "The impact was on the rear, where no one was seated."

"But the gunfire?"

I didn't have an answer to that. Perhaps they didn't hit anything on purpose, but my expertise in gun fights was limited to the last two days. I had to assume these two had a better working knowledge of such things.

"Okay, I don't know about that," I admitted. "But if she's after me for any reason, wouldn't I make the best bait?"

"Harvey, we can't do that to you."

"Chase, going through El Tigre might be the only way to find out what is going on with Victoria. I'll go looking for her one way or the other." I puffed my chest out like I was still a twenty-year-old kid in the Navy.

I watched Chase look at Velazquez as if he was seeking someone to talk sense into me. The enforcer shook his head, saying, "Doesn't matter to me if he gets himself killed."

"How many men does she have working for her?" Chase asked Velazquez.

"It can't be too many," he admitted.

"All we need is one, then," Chase said. "We can interrogate him. Can you help?" He directed the question to Esteban Velazquez.

"I need El Tigre—the girl after," he stated.

"As long as she gets me to Victoria," I agreed before Chase could respond. I wasn't sure what Velazquez would do with El Tigre if he got her, but it didn't matter. I needed to find Victoria before something happened to her. "How do we do this?"

Chase let out a heavy sigh. "I doubt there were only the two men in the other car. They know we went to ground before the cops swarmed in. I bet if we wanted to find them, we could just stroll out onto the street."

"What about the police?" I asked. "They'll be all over the Suburban, won't they?"

"Oh, yeah," Chase said. "The best thing we can do is ignore them. You and I go out together. With the police around, they won't make another head-on attack right here. If we can set the stage for them instead, they could easily take the bait."

"Where?" Velazquez asked.

Chase glanced out the window. "It's getting dark. Let's lead them south to South Cove."

"What's South Cove?" I asked.

"It's a little natural area with a boardwalk to preserve a very tiny portion of the natural area in Lake Worth. It's not big, but there's only one way on and off the boardwalk."

"Won't that make us the proverbial fish in a barrel?" I asked.

"That's where Esteban comes in," he said. "He'll close off their retreat."

I didn't love the idea, but if I was going to get to El Tigre, this seemed like the fastest method. I took a deep breath. "Let's do this."

"*¡Loco viejo!*" Velazquez muttered as he shook his head.

"Wait, Harvey." Chase grabbed my arm as I started down the steps of the stairwell where we had retreated.

"What?" I winced as I jerked by arm away.

"You need a gun." He stuck his hand out to take the 9mm back from Velazquez.

"Do you have one?" I asked the Cuban.

He pulled the side of his jacket back to reveal a silver Colt pistol with an ornately carved handle.

"Does it have notches for people you killed?"

"It's not big enough." Esteban was not amused.

I swallowed and started back down the stairs.

"Does he know where he is going?" Velazquez asked Chase.

I paused and looked back at the bartender and the enforcer, realizing in my haste I didn't have a clue where I was.

"I guess you should lead, Chase," I told him. "I've never actually been to Palm Beach."

"First lesson: this is West Palm. The folks across the lake would have a conniption fit if they thought you mistook this hovel for their town."

"Oh, sorry."

When he grinned, Chase looked like a kid. "Oh, it doesn't bother us. Neither of us is from Florida."

Chase skipped two steps and opened the door leading us down a service hallway into the alley we fled up earlier.

Six police cars cordoned off Flagler Drive around the smashed Suburban. A white van was parked in the middle of the street. The words "Crime Scene Mobile Investigation" were emblazoned on the side.

"Let's head south." Chase picked up the pace. "Try to be a little curious about what happened."

"Why?" I asked. "Don't we want to just sneak by?"

"We do, and the first thing that will look out of place is a couple of guys trying not to pay attention to a scene like that."

"Oh, makes sense."

As we walked on the sidewalk, my head swiveled as I tried to look at everything. As we passed a park with strange sculptures resembling small obelisks with round glass balls embedded in each of them, I wished Martha could see them. The dream of traveling to places all along the coast had made her want to go cruising.

Despite the danger I was about to face, I didn't feel any fear. Only sadness filling my heart.

For a split second, I didn't care if El Tigre or the Sandoval Cartel killed me. At least I wouldn't face another day on this planet without Martha. She'd be mad at me, though. My job right now was to save Victoria, and if Martha thought I'd given up on that, she'd be disappointed.

I gathered my resolve and increased my gait to keep up with Chase.

After a couple of blocks, we crossed Flagler. The traffic was bumper-to-bumper as the police tried to clear the scene down the street.

"Do you think they're following us?" I asked.

"I spotted one."

"Do you think he'll give her up if we catch him, Chase?"

"Hard to say. Loyalty isn't something that's easy to buy. Most people will eventually turn on an employer if the right kind of pressure is applied."

"Would Esteban turn on his employer?" I asked.

"Scar? No, that wouldn't happen. He might withhold something if it does hurt his boss, but he'd never betray him."

"Do you trust him?" I asked.

"Truthfully, Harvey, Scar is one of the most trustworthy people I know. Sure, he'd kill both of us if his boss told him to, but if he says something, you can trust him to do it."

"What if he says he is going to kill you?" I asked as Chase maneuvered around me so that he was walking next to the curb. The transition was subtle, and at first, I didn't realize what he'd done.

"Oh, I'd run for the hills, because that bastard means it."

"I'll try to stay on his good side."

We passed a small rectangular brown sign reading "South Cove."

"Follow me." Chase stepped onto the boardwalk that jutted out from the shore. In the dark, I could barely make out the silhouette of the railing against the faint lights of Palm Beach on the opposite shore of Lake Worth. The bridge was new, or at least a fairly recent structure.

I followed him as we strolled out. What was El Tigre's man thinking? It had to be odd that we ventured out here in the dark. Would he think we were meeting someone? So far, the woman had interfered every time I'd come into contact with someone trying to help me. If that brazen attitude continued, there would be someone coming along soon.

"Okay, Harvey," Chase whispered. "The water isn't deep, but the sharks like to hunt up here at night."

"Sharks?"

"Yeah, they don't want to eat you. But that won't stop them from accidentally taking a chunk out of you. Most likely they'll just sweep your legs and scare the piss out of you."

"Great," I said. "So stay out of the water?"

"Well ..." He thought for a moment. "Until you need to get in the water."

"Why would I need to get in the water, Chase?"

"Because it beats getting shot."

"Is this like the electric current around the dock?" I asked, hoping he was exaggerating the presence of sharks.

"No, there really are sharks out there. They might not bother you, but don't think they aren't there."

I let out a groan.

"Don't worry, I've been face to face with more than a few sharks. I've yet to be bitten."

"Maybe they are scared of you," I pointed out.

"They should be," he whispered, and I could tell he was smiling in the dark.

We stopped somewhere in the middle of the boardwalk. While the ambient glow of streetlights and neon signs let me make out the railing running along the edge of the walkway, I couldn't distinguish where the boardwalk actually touched the shore.

"We have company," Chase said under his breath.

I scanned the spot where I thought the shore connected, but I couldn't make out anyone.

"I don't see anything," I told him.

"He's there. Wait, I think we have another one coming."

"You sure it's not Esteban?"

"Too soon," he told me. "And too short."

"What's the play?" I asked.

"One more."

Three? I was hoping for one or two. After seeing Chase in action, I figured he could handle two. If not, Velazquez would swoop in like backup. Three, though, might be more than even Chase could handle before Velazquez showed up.

"Two more," Chase said.

"Five?" I stopped walking. "Can you call Esteban? Get him to come in early."

"If you have a phone."

"I lost mine," I said. "Don't you have one?"

"I don't carry one," he confessed.

"What are we going to do?"

"Let's hope they want to take you alive," Chase said. "I want you to move to the end of the pier. Be ready to go over if you need to."

I swallowed hard, reconsidering the plan. This was a means to an end, I told myself. Victoria was the only objective.

I shuffled backward along the boardwalk. Chase seemed to be

swallowed up in the shadows as I distanced myself from him. The shoreline was almost impossible to see. Where was Velazquez?

"How's it going?" Chase said in the dark.

There was a response followed by the sounds of a struggle. A flash of light and a muffled bang broke through the night.

The gun fired twice, and I dropped to the deck as the men between Chase and the shore returned fire. I couldn't see Chase anymore, but shapes were moving down the boardwalk. Would someone report the gunfire? On the water, the sound would carry, but it might be hard to pinpoint the direction it came from. Unless someone actually saw the fight, it wasn't likely the police would show up any time soon.

Besides, I wasn't sure police involvement would help Victoria. If she had gotten in over her head, she might be facing legal troubles along with whatever dangers she was up against.

The boardwalk went quiet. I tried to see what was going on, but everything seemed still. Then I heard footsteps. Was it Chase? If I called out and it wasn't, they'd know where I was.

I glanced over my shoulder at the water. Sharks—or whatever—were coming down the walkway. At least in the water, I could move up onto the small islands and stay out of sight. Sharks can't walk, right?

With a sudden resolve, I scaled over the railing and dropped into the water. My feet sloshed through the muddy bottom. I expected sand, but instead it was a mixture of mud and sand that created a sludge-like footing. As my feet sank into it, the methane trapped under the silt escaped in a noxious stream. Without paying any attention, I waded through the water away from the wooden structure. My eyes focused on the mount of grass and scrubs rising above the water's surface.

It was only thirty feet away, and I felt a sigh of relief when I stepped out of the lake and onto dry land.

"Harvey?" a voice called from the dark.

"Chase?" I answered.

"What are you doing over there?" he asked.

"I was trying to get away," I said. "I figured if I got onto the island I wouldn't have to worry about sharks. They can't walk, right?" My quip was an attempt to seem less scared.

Another voice chuckled. I recognized Velazquez as he said, "Gators do, though."

I glanced around the island, suddenly realizing I hadn't considered alligators.

23

SHAMELESS
DOUGLAS PRATT

NOW THAT THE island didn't feel as safe, I was less worried about the sharks. I waded back across the expanse in calf-deep water. I pulled up over the railing. My knee ached from the fall I'd taken the other day. It felt like a lifetime ago that I'd met Troy on another dock.

"I'm going to clear the walkway," Velazquez said before vanishing into the dark.

Crouched in the corner at the end of the boardwalk was a Latino man. His face was swelling, but I guessed he was in his late twenties.

"Alright, buddy," Chase said to him, grabbing him by the lapel of his black jacket. He pulled the man to his feet. The guy was clutching his side, and even in the faint light, I could see black liquid oozing between the fingers.

"He's shot?"

"Yeah, it's not good, either," Chase said. "Which is why he's going to tell us what we want to know so we can get an ambulance out here."

The man seemed to understand what was expected. He nodded vigorously.

"You're up, Harvey," Chase told me.

I studied the man. What questions was I supposed to ask?

"Where is El Tigre?" I asked.

The injured killer stared up at me. He shook his head. In a strained tone, he replied, "She's going to kill Mendoza."

I glanced up at Chase. My face must have shown the fear that flashed through me. What about Victoria?

"Where is she going to do this?" Chase asked as I fell silent.

"Down in Biscayne Bay," the man muttered. "*Necessito un hospital, por favor.*"

"Soon," Chase promised. "Where in the bay?"

"I don't know," he said. "Where those old buildings are. You know, it was some kind of town the Mafia built out there to hide from the government."

"Stiltsville," Chase said.

"What's that?" I asked him.

"It's a group of buildings—or rather, ruins of them. They're down in the south of the bay."

"Is the Mafia still there?" I asked.

Chase shook his head. "No, it's just an old site. There are still some structures out there, but no one lives in them. Supposedly there was some gambling out there in the thirties, but nowadays the rangers probably chase away more vagrants than anything."

"Please get me some help," the man begged.

"Come on, Harvey," Chase said. "We need to be gone before the ambulance arrives."

He knelt in front of the wounded thug. "Help will be here soon. I'd suggest you skip warning your boss. She might not appreciate your weakness."

Esteban grumbled something in Spanish. I guessed he didn't approve of helping the man. It was a stark difference between Chase and Esteban. I'd seen them both kill in the last few hours, but Chase seemed remorseful, even if there wasn't another option. Maybe I'd call it a more human reaction. Or he held more respect for life. I don't know, but it was admirable.

"Give me your phone," Chase said to Esteban as they walked toward shore.

"He can identify us," the enforcer pointed out.

"Just give me your phone."

Esteban Velazquez handed an older flip phone to him. Chase dialed 911 and reported an injured man on the boardwalk. When he handed the phone back to Esteban, the man flung it out into the water and said, "Perfectly good waste of a phone."

"Okay, we need to get a boat." Chase ignored Esteban's snide comment.

"Don't you have a boat?" he asked Chase.

"It's too slow," Chase said.

"Give me half an hour. We can meet down at El Cid."

Chase gave him a nod as we reached the street. Esteban crossed Flagler and disappeared.

"Come on." Chase pulled me along. "We need some distance between us and this scene."

"Where's El Cid?"

"South of Royal Park Bridge. There's a historic area there, but they have a dock. I'm guessing that's where Scar will want to meet."

It didn't take but a couple of blocks to realize I was holding Chase back. The man could have jogged the entire way, but this old man with a bum knee was hobbling along at quarter speed. Quarter speed for the former Marine—for me, it felt like I was double-timing it.

We hiked along in silence. I didn't have much to say. But my brain was working overtime. If El Tigre planned to kill Mendoza, Victoria could find herself in the crosshairs too.

"You're awfully quiet, Harvey," Chase said after a few minutes.

"To tell the truth, Chase, I'm worried."

"About your daughter?" he asked.

"Of course. Do you have kids?"

"No, I don't. They don't seem to be in the cards for me right now."

"That's what Martha and I thought too," I told him. "Until we found Victoria."

"What happened to Martha?" he asked. "If that's not too personal, that is."

"It's okay," I replied. "She was killed in a car accident. The cops presumed it was a drunk driver, but they fled the scene."

"I'm sorry, Harvey."

"Wish I could say it's okay. Certainly not your fault. I just miss her."

"I understand." Chase squeezed my shoulder. "At least, I guess I do."

In the distance, the rumble of a motor came down the lake. The wake from a large Baja sloshed against the shoreline. It was inconsiderate of the driver, as his wake was pounding anything tied up at the nearby docks.

The driver hadn't illuminated his navigation lights, either.

Chase let out a groan as the boat slowed down near the pier at El Cid.

"Is that him?" I asked.

"I think so. Come on. The idiot doesn't know anything about boats."

He jogged ahead, leaving me to attempt to keep up. By the time I reached the dock, Chase had pulled the Baja over to the side and tied it off. It was a thirty-six-foot boat with a bright red finish that looked like it came right off the showroom floor.

"Why don't you let me drive?" Chase said to Velazquez. "I don't want the Coast Guard or FWP to pull us over."

Esteban raised his hands off the helm. "I only acquire the boat. You can steer it." He slid out of the captain's chair and plopped into the other seat.

"How long will it take us to get there?" I asked.

"If we can get out the pass, it will be a lot faster," Chase explained. "Still a couple of hours, though."

I wasted no time stepping off the dock and dropping onto the sole. "What can I do?" I asked.

Chase followed me into the boat, pulling the one dock line with him. He shoved the Baja away from the dock as he pushed the throttle forward.

"We can't rip through here," he told us. "It would draw the attention of everyone. I'm guessing this boat wasn't just borrowed."

Esteban shrugged. "No one is looking for it," he assured us in a less than reassuring tone.

When I'd come down the coast, I skipped around this area. I'd anchored north of St. Augustine but didn't stop again until I was in Fort Lauderdale. It didn't look much different from Fort Lauderdale or Miami. Condominiums towered along the eastern and western shorelines of Lake Worth. Anchor lights dotted the dark waters, and a glittering array of city lights reminded me I was still in civilization.

None of this was the dream we had when Martha and I started down this path. We envisioned desolate islands with crystal-clear waters filled with fish and dolphins.

When Chase finally exited the lake into the Atlantic Ocean, the night sky loomed over us from the east. Behind us, the glow of Palm Beach beckoned us back to the protected waterway.

As if we had passed a physical threshold, the Atlantic immediately tossed three- to four-foot waves at us. Nothing too big, and Chase pressed the throttle down to speed through them. He studied the glowing screen from the chartplotter. It was too dark to read the water, and he was relying on the navigation system to keep him in safer waters. Unlike some of the areas in the Keys, it didn't take long for the ocean floor to sink deep beneath us. Within minutes, the depth gauge registered eighty-eight feet. A hundred and seventy-five. Five-hundred and sixty-six.

By now, Chase had the twin 540 HP engines screaming at full speed. The hull barely bounced on the small waves as it sliced over the tops. The navigation screen indicated we were clipping along in the dark at just over seventy knots per hour. Chase maintained a vigilant lookout for any lights that might be in our path.

I glanced over at Esteban, who seemed unmoved by the entire affair. If it weren't for the wind whipping his hair around, he could have been sitting at the bar watching a baseball game.

We continued south, and after ten minutes I found myself staring at the changing coastline as the Baja carried us past an endless line of coastal cities. After several miles, I turned my attention to the other direction to admire the vast universe that opened up over the ocean.

After some time, the drone of the engine combined with the exhaustion of the past few days led my eyes to close slowly. I opened them in what felt like only a few moments. The engine throttled back, and the Baja slowed.

"What's going on?" I asked, straightening up and trying to find my bearings.

"We're almost to Stiltsville," Chase said. "I'm going dark."

"What time is it?" I noticed the sky was lightening in the east. Time lately seemed to pass on its own accord. I had been running for days, and the logical passing of the second hand never felt consistent.

"Almost four-thirty," he said. Not 0430. I wondered how long it had taken him to transition from military time. My time in the Navy was short-lived enough I never got accustomed to using the twenty-four-hour format.

"Southeast," Esteban called. He was standing up, looking through a pair of binoculars. Chase and I followed the trajectory of his finger to see a light in the distance. "Is this Mendoza's yacht?"

He handed the binoculars to Chase, who took a look. "Appears so. What do you think, Harvey?"

He passed them to me. When I peered through them, I could make out the lights and shape of the vessel, but there was no way I could make a distinct identification of it. "I don't know. Maybe?"

"I think so," Chase agreed. "The dinghy on the back is in the same place."

"How far is it?" I asked.

"About three miles."

"Looks like they have company too," Esteban said. "Another boat heading toward them."

"El Tigre?" I asked.

"Seems likely," the drug enforcer responded.

My worry for Victoria's safety increased. "What do we do?"

"I guess we interfere." Chase glanced at Esteban.

"You are good at that. But what's the plan?"

"If she's there to kill Mendoza, we need to get between them."

"I don't care if Mendoza dies." Esteban snorted.

"But Victoria is there." I hated the pleading note in my voice, but I wasn't too proud to beg.

"Alright, we get between El Tigre and Victoria," Chase said. "Esteban wants El Tigre. While he's going after her, Harvey, you need to get to Victoria. I'll back you up."

I nodded, and Chase rammed the throttle forward. The bow of the Baja lifted for a few seconds as the boat leveled out on plane.

The cigarette boat ripped through the darkness as I peered at the lights of Mendoza's yacht and the intersecting red and green navigation lights on the other boat. As the Baja covered the gap between us and them, the yacht's features grew more distinct. The other boat reached the stern of the yacht. I couldn't hear the gunshots over the roar of the twin motors, but the flashes in the dark alerted us to the impending battle.

"Ready!" Chase shouted when we were a hundred yards out. It wasn't a question—more of a command.

I checked the 9mm. Was I ready to shoot someone? I wasn't sure. All I knew was how much I wanted to hug Victoria and protect her. I couldn't let Martha down.

Chase twisted the wheel to port as he pulled the throttle back. The sudden deceleration combined with the change in direction slid the Baja into the side of the yacht with nothing more than a *thunk* and maybe some scuffing of both boats' gel coats.

Before I realized we had stopped, Esteban bounded off the gunwale of the Baja and over the railing of Mendoza's boat.

"Stay behind me," Chase ordered as he followed the enforcer.

I scrambled after him. As I grabbed the railing, I glanced back to see the other boat. Two men fired automatic weapons at several of Mendoza's men, who took cover at the aft of the yacht.

Esteban's gun popped, and I turned as a man tumbled off the deck above us.

"Move!" he shouted toward us. Esteban inched along the edge of the railing toward the rear of the boat.

"But Victoria—"

"Harvey, we're going forward." Chase grabbed my arm. "Stay behind me."

"Got it!"

I glanced over my shoulder to see Esteban firing down on Mendoza's men. He wanted El Tigre, and she had to get aboard before he could get to her. Of course, it also brought her and her men closer to my Vic.

My attention turned back to Chase, who moved along the narrow edge between the cabin and the railing. I trusted he knew what he was doing, but I tightened my grip on the 9mm just the same.

The gunfire on the back of the boat stopped. Chase moved as if he hadn't noticed the change, and except for a slight tilt of his head, I might not have known he'd even noticed it. Instead, he climbed up the cabin to the flybridge. I struggled to follow him, but after several tries, I clambered up after him. Chase had already descended the steps into the cabin as I made it over the helm.

Gunfire erupted from below, and Chase shouted, "Stay back, Harvey!"

The entire boat shuddered, and I felt an almost imperceptible list to starboard. I dropped to my knees, taking cover behind the captain's chair. The cushioned seat would do little to protect me from gunfire. But for now, the volley of bullets seemed directed elsewhere. I couldn't tell where.

"Stop him!" Chase shouted. "He's got Victoria."

When I heard that I bounded to my feet. I straightened to see Mendoza dragging Victoria toward the Baja. He held her up like a shield.

"I'll kill her!" he shouted.

Chase had his 45 pointed at the two. Esteban was swinging his weapon back and forth between Mendoza and a dark-haired woman who was holding a rifle pointed at Mendoza. Everything was moving too fast, yet somehow it seemed in slow motion.

"I'm serious!" Mendoza clutched Victoria.

The woman, who I presumed was El Tigre, screamed, "I'll kill you!"

"She'll still be dead."

"Your boss won't like that," El Tigre said. "Once he finds out you killed his daughter."

His daughter? I was confused.

There wasn't time to think about it as Mendoza pulled Victoria closer to him, eliminating any clean shot.

"Sandoval long stopped worrying about his offspring." Mendoza sneered at El Tigre.

Victoria struggled, but the bigger man pulled his forearm tighter around her throat, subduing her. My stomach roiled with fire, and I raised the 9mm.

"Victoria!" Her eyes shifted up to me. She mouthed something.

"Don't move, Mendoza," El Tigre said.

Mendoza shouted, and I shifted my eyes in that second to El Tigre.

"Don't do it!" Chase shouted at her before directing an order to Esteban. "Stop her."

"I don't know what you expect me to do differently. I can't kill her."

El Tigre flashed a wicked grin when he said that—as if she just got permission for something. There wasn't anything they could do except kill her, and Esteban Velazquez had just told her that wouldn't happen.

I twisted around and fired toward her. "I can!"

The bullets weren't close, but instinct caused her to return fire. I felt the bullet hit my shoulder, spinning me around. I slammed into the deck of the bridge. The wound stung, and I had a feeling it would do a lot more in a bit.

Get up and fight, Harvey, I ordered myself.

Pushing up, saw El Tigre lying on the swim platform. Did I hit her?

The Baja roared as the twin engines engaged. The wash from the wake rocked the yacht, and I turned to see it racing away with Mendoza at the wheel. There was no sign of Victoria.

"Victoria!" I tried to climb down the steps to the lower deck.

"She's gone, *viejo*," Esteban snapped.

"Gone? What do you mean?"

"Mendoza has her," Chase said. "He dragged her aboard."

I shook my head.

"Damned fool," Esteban growled. "He got away because of you."

"She was going to kill Victoria," I said.

He shook his head and walked to the wounded woman.

"It's okay, Harvey," Chase said. "You were right. She was about to pull the trigger."

"What about Victoria?" I asked. "That didn't look like a couple of lovers."

Chase nodded. "No, it didn't."

Behind the yacht, the small runabout El Tigre had come on was smoking, riddled with bullets. Three bodies slumped over the front.

"It's superficial." Esteban looked up from the woman. "Good thing the old man can't shoot straight."

"I wasn't trying to hit her," I said. "I just wanted her to take cover."

Esteban scoffed.

"Besides, she got one into me." I pointed to my shoulder.

Esteban stood up and looked at my shoulder. "She grazed you, that's all."

"Grazed me? It hurts like hell."

"That's good," Chase said.

El Tigre was sitting up, holding her side. The bullet passed through her, missing anything vital.

"You!" I turned on her. "What did you mean when you said she was Sandoval's daughter?"

The dark-haired woman stared up at me. She was only a little older than Victoria. Her eyes looked familiar somehow.

"She's his daughter. I was trying to stop him."

I shook my head. "No, she's not. Her father was a federal agent. How could Victoria be Sandoval's daughter?"

The woman smiled. "You're right. I made that up."

"What do you mean?" I questioned.

"Gordon, do you smell that?" Esteban asked Chase.

The former Marine nodded. "I'll check it out."

I barely registered their conversation as I tried to understand what this killer was telling me.

"Who is she, then?" I had to know.

"She's who you think she is, mostly," El Tigre said.

"What?"

"I'm Isabella, Sandoval's daughter. I hoped Mendoza would buy the bluff. At least long enough to get your daughter back, but I guess it doesn't matter anymore. It seems my father hates me now as much as I hate him. When we escaped his house, we switched identities. She wanted away from her father. I wanted revenge."

"Switched?" I questioned. "That makes you—why are you after Victoria?"

"I helped her escape my father. She got away because that idiot Mendoza went after me instead."

"That doesn't explain anything."

"I risked my own escape so your daughter could get away. My father had butchered her parents when her father got too close. He was going to kill her too. I realized I had to save Isabella, I mean, Victoria. I helped her escape," the woman explained. "Now after all that, she's back in, and it's my one shot to get close enough to kill my father."

I stepped back, leaning against the railing. "How? You were going to shoot her."

She shook her head. "No, she was supposed to hand Mendoza over. We were going to use him to get to my father. Something must have gone wrong. Her cover was blown, I guess."

"She was working with you?" I stammered in disbelief.

"Ever since someone killed her mother," she replied. "She believed Sandoval had found her."

"Her mother? Martha?"

The woman nodded. "Sandoval, my father, never actually found her, but your wife must have been digging around in something. Attracted his attention."

"She was killed in a car accident," I said.

She shook her head again.

Chase charged out of the cabin. "We have to get off the boat." Everyone stared at him but didn't move.

Now I noticed the smell—smoke.

He began operating the windlass to lower the dinghy. "Come on. Let's get into the dinghy."

As the smell of smoke increased, I glanced back to see black clouds billowing out of the cabin.

"Esteban, can you manage her?" Chase asked, nodding his head toward the injured woman.

"Yeah." Esteban helped El Tigre to her feet before lifting her over into the dinghy.

Chase warned us, "This is going to be crowded."

Esteban gave the little boat a once-over. "There's no motor."

The enforcer was correct. The dinghy had a place on the transom for an outboard, but no engine was attached.

"It's probably been removed and stored somewhere," I said. A lot of cruisers don't travel with a motor attached. It might be stored on deck or below in an engine room.

"No time to look for it." Chase helped me to climb aboard.

Once I was settled on the rear seat next to Esteban, Chase stepped aboard and pushed the ten-foot boat away from the swim platform.

The smoke darkened the lights still glowing in the cabin, and after a few moments, I saw the first tongues of fire reaching out.

We drifted farther away as the yacht began to glow orange in the dark Atlantic night.

PART IV

STEVEN BECKER

Always looking for a new location or adventure to write about, Steven Becker can usually be found on or near the water. He splits his time between Tampa and the Florida Keys - paddling, sailing, diving, fishing or exploring.

Find out more by visiting www.stevenbeckerauthor.com or contact me directly at booksbybecker@gmail.com.

24

SHAMELESS
STEVEN BECKER

WHEN THE YACHT BLEW, it illuminated the sky for a long second before the flaming debris fell to the water around us. With only a flimsy pair of oars to escape the scene, we were lucky not to take a direct hit. Chase paddled the small boat far enough away from danger, though we could still feel the pull of the vortex as the yacht sunk.

I lay with my head against the soft-sided gunwales by the bow, holding my balled-up shirt against my shoulder. Chase continued to row away from the conflagration. I turned to see he was heading toward one of the derelict buildings. Several more lurked in the background, illuminated by the flaming remains of the yacht.

He coasted to the dock of the closest and called for Estaben to tie us off to one of the pilings.

"We can't stay here," the enforcer said. "At least me or her." He jerked his head in the direction of El Tigre.

I raised my head. "Forget that. I need to see this through. Isabella saved me from Sandoval, I want to return the favor."

"And kill everyone in the process." Esteban smirked. "The patron wants you. That is my job." He raised his hands like maybe he understood, but it wouldn't deter him from his duty.

Though El Tigre might be an asset, I also knew she was a loose cannon. The name alone said as much. If Esteban wanted to take her to his boss, I would not interfere. I looked at Chase. "What do you think?"

"I think we need to have a look at that shoulder. Check in that hold you're sitting on and see if there's a first aid kit."

Esteban glanced to the northeast. The lights of downtown Miami were clearly visible. "*Mi amigo*, we can spit on Miami from here. First responders will be here any minute."

Even with Jay Delp covering for Chase, there were a whole lot of bodies marking our trail from Palm Beach County. I'm sure Estaben and El Tigre were probably wanted as well. After they had helped me, I felt I owed them their freedom.

"Leave me here and go hide in one of the other houses. I'll cover for you." I slid over and opened the hold. Inside was some safety gear, which I removed. There was no first aid kit. Fortunately, the dock was built low to the water, and I was able to sidle onto its rough surface. Once my butt was planted on the warped boards, I kicked out with my legs and pushed the dinghy away.

"Good luck, Harvey. You need me, call the hotel," Chase said.

"Thanks, all of you." My eye was drawn to El Tigre. There was something about her expression that told me I hadn't seen the last of her. I watched as Chase rowed the dinghy away, waiting until the darkness enveloped the small boat.

I sat on the dock holding my shirt to my shoulder and tried to catch my breath. A few minutes later, I heard the rotors of a helicopter. Then the chopper's spotlight broke through the darkness, scanning the water where the debris still smoldered. The chopper hovered over the area, its brilliant light sweeping the surface searching for survivors. Another minute later I saw the red and green bow-lights of several boats approaching.

One reached the area quickly. Surprisingly, it was a smaller boat. Miles from shore, my only way out was to get attention by using one of the flares I'd found in the safety gear. I had concocted a story of sorts while I waited. Hoping it would hold up under the interrogation

I would likely face, I twisted off the top of the red hand flare and pulled the short cord.

Smoke streamed from the tube, then a bright red glow appeared. I waved it back and forth trying to attract the attention of the small boat. The chopper must have noticed the light and the smoke and directed its beam in my direction. In the process, it illuminated the small boat, which was a center console with a National Park Service logo on the bow. I waved the flare in the direction of the man at the helm.

I released a pent-up breath when he saw me and sped toward the dock. Just before he reached the structure he pulled back on the throttle and coasted up to one of the pilings.

"Are you okay?" he called across.

"Shoulder wound, but yes." I wasn't about to tell him it was a gunshot wound until I was forced to.

"Anyone else?"

"Just me. I haven't seen any other survivors."

"From the look of the explosion, I'd say you were lucky."

"You saw it?" I'd wondered how he reached the scene before the two larger fireboats had pulled up to the wreckage. Another, larger center-console was just arriving as well.

"Kurt Hunter, special agent in charge of the park." He reached a hand across and helped me aboard his boat.

"Harvey Thackerson." I held my shirt over my wounded shoulder.

"You need to have that looked at?" he asked as he idled away from the stilt house.

There was no denying the pain, but I had the bleeding under control. I knew that hospitals were required to report gunshot wounds and decided I could wait. "No."

I was waiting for his next question when another boat pulled alongside. Blue-and white-lights strobed from its T-top, illuminating us. "Hunter? What are you doing out at night?" The man behind the wheel called over, his smirk evident.

I saw the agent tense up. Instead of returning the obvious insult, he took the high road. "Got a survivor. Only one I've seen."

The men aboard the Miami-Dade police boat must have gotten the message. "Right. We'll check around."

"I'm going to run him in to get his shoulder looked after. Think you can handle this?"

He pointed to the two boats that had just arrived. "With those babies? We got this."

We all turned to see the pair of fireboats shooting streams of water onto the debris field, which was all that remained of the yacht. Hunter pressed down on the throttle and started to move away from the scene, saying something under his breath about boat envy that I didn't catch. I was pretty sure it had something to do with the Miami-Dade response—probably some kind of interagency squabble.

With the massive power of the fire boats what remained of the blaze was quickly extinguished. We had moved about a quarter mile from the scene when Hunter stopped the boat.

"I'll need a statement."

"Sure."

He hesitated. "Where can I drop you?"

That was a good question, and one I hadn't considered when relieving Chase of any obligation to me. Looking around, I could clearly see the lights of downtown Miami. From there the glow extended south, outlining the mainland past where we were. I tried to recall the geography from my trip to Key West. I'd had good weather and stayed offshore, but barely remembered the charts.

I had nowhere to go and no way to pick up the breadcrumbs from the Baja with Mendoza and Victoria aboard that had escaped before the explosion. I thought they went south, but they could have just headed in that direction to escape the blaze, then circled back to Miami.

At this point, I was as lost as I'd been since tracking down Victoria in Key West. I glanced over at Hunter, wondering if I could trust him. So far, everyone I had crossed paths with had aided me, but he was law enforcement—though if I had the choice between dealing with the Miami police or a Park Service agent, it would be the agent.

"If you have someplace we could talk for a while, I've got a story to tell." I could tell he was interested.

"The park headquarters is close, but it's in the middle of nowhere. Do you have someone you can call?"

"Yes." I lied.

"Alright. Hold on."

We sped across the bay, moving through an area where he slowed and shone a light to catch the triangular and square markers defining a channel. I glanced down at the chartplotter, recalling the feature that I had purposefully avoided on my trip south. Once we were clear, he changed course and headed to a dark spot on the mainland.

After cruising past several miles of mangrove-lined shores, we entered a long channel. Just before we reached a boat ramp he turned again into a small side channel. The law enforcement presence was clear here, with a tricked-out ICE boat and several FWC boats. There were also a few smaller Park Service boats in a nearby marina.

Hunter slid the center console into a slip and tied off the boat. Once we were secure, he shut off the engine and stepped up to the dock. He reached a hand down to help, which I shook off, not wanting to appear injured.

I followed him to a two-story building next to what looked like a large maintenance shed. He pulled out a keychain, found the key, and unlocked the door.

"Hold on. I'll get the lights."

I waited by the door.

"We can go upstairs to the conference room." He turned to me.

This was the first time he'd gotten a good look at me and I caught his expression. From what I could see of myself in the reflection of the glass doors, it wasn't a pretty sight.

"Get you a water or something? Probably need to have a look at that shoulder, too."

"That would be good."

He went to a small room that I guessed was a kitchen and returned with two bottles of water and a first aid kit. I followed him upstairs, wondering how I was going to enlist his help—or at this point, stay out of jail.

"Let's have a look at that shoulder, then."

"Maybe you ought to hear my story first." I was worried the gunshot wound would change things.

"No matter. You can talk while I work." He moved toward me.

There was no choice except to let him look. I grimaced as I pulled my shirt away, not sure what to expect. The blood had dried somewhat, but it was clear the bullet had just grazed my shoulder. To me, the channel running across my skin looked like I'd been shot, but to someone else, it might not.

"This is going to sting." He applied some hydrogen peroxide to a wad of cotton and gently rubbed it against the wound.

It did sting, but with the injuries I'd already sustained to my head, elbow, and knee I was used to the pain. If anything it cleared my head. He tossed the old wad into the garbage and repeated the process. Finally, he was satisfied and covered the spot with a bandage.

"I'd see a doctor if I were you. Don't think you need stitches, but there's always a risk of infection."

I nodded and took a sip of water. "Thanks."

He pulled a pen and a small notebook from his pocket. "Okay."

"This started a while before the explosion." I went into the story. He wrote furiously as I told him my entire story, from Victoria's adoption to when he picked me up. I did leave out a few details about some of the people who helped along the way, though.

Hunter was quiet for a long minute. I leaned back in the chair and sipped water while I waited for his verdict.

"Where do you want to go with this? Far as I can see, you haven't committed any crime. There's no reason to hold you."

"I want my daughter back."

He was quiet for another minute. "There's someone I know in Key Largo who might be able to help."

I looked at the guy, wondering what a park ranger could do that Chase, Kate, or Troy couldn't. Not that I was in any condition to complain.

My body ached. Elbow, knee, head, and now my shoulder. The injuries were mounting. Added to the aches from years of hauling furniture through the store, I wasn't sure how much longer I could keep this up.

Thoughts of my wife and daughter were like a lifeline. The only reason I could continue and see this through, wherever it led.

"I'd appreciate that."

25

SHAMELESS
STEVEN BECKER

STANDING on the dock in Key Largo, I felt like I was being shuttled around instead of gaining ground. Kurt Hunter was another in a growing list of people who had taken up my cause. I understood his inability to help outside his territory. As a law enforcement officer, he had no choice. But after putting me up for the night with one of his agents in a Park Service house on Adams Key, I trusted him.

He introduced me to Alicia Phon, who he had proclaimed was a tech wizard. Along with her boyfriend, TJ, they ran a diving charter. I wondered how those skills transferred, but I guessed I'd find out.

Alicia led us upstairs to their residence above the dive shop. We entered what was essentially an apartment and stopped beside a pair of French doors. When the lights came on, I realized that their diving business was just a sideline.

The entire wall facing the entrance was filled with large, flat-screen monitors. She moved to a workstation that appeared pretty austere. What caught my eye as she started pecking at her keyboard was the captain's chair that occupied the center of the room. It could have come off the Starship Enterprise.

"That's TJ's. He calls this the war room," Alicia said. "Rico Mendoza was the man's name, right?"

She wasn't one for small talk. "Yes, and the Sandoval Cartel."

At some point, I wanted to get a look at the Sandoval family tree and see if I could figure out if El Tigre had been honest when she said that Victoria wasn't Sandoval's daughter. That would wait, though. First I had to find her.

Several of the displays illuminated simultaneously showing a headshot of Mendoza. Another screen showed his public record, which was spread across three monitors, allowing the text to be readable from across the room.

"Record has nothing unusual."

I scanned the document showing several arrests, mostly years ago when he was younger. There was nothing in the last decade. Another document appeared, this one on CIA letterhead.

"Known associates."

Seeing the top-secret moniker made the room go quiet. The only sound was the cool air flowing in through some ducts cut into the ceiling. I noticed the war room was cooler than the rest of the house, probably intentionally to protect the equipment from the Florida heat and humidity. After spending most of the last few months aboard boats, I had to say it felt refreshing. We all read through the list. The names meant nothing to me. The next page showed an organizational chart of the cartel with Mendoza's name on the second tier.

Kurt moved over to the wall and pointed to one of the names. "Jose Nanches. Sounds familiar. Can you see what you have on him?"

Alicia nodded and went to work. Another two screens populated. "Looks like he's head of a group that owns several high-end resorts."

A minute later a list of the company's assets showed on another screen. I scanned the list. "This one's in the Keys. Little Palm Island Resort and Spa."

"Damn. This is starting to make sense," Alicia said.

Before I could ask what she saw that I hadn't, the door opened. Light from the residence temporarily washed out the screens.

"Hey, Kurt."

Two men entered the room. The first thing I noticed about the first was his hair, or rather, his dreadlocks. He was a burly man dressed in cargo shorts and an open Hawaiian shirt. His smile seemed like it was a permanent fixture. He embraced Kurt with a bear hug. The other man was thinner and much better dressed. A client, I guessed.

"Harvey, this is TJ and ..." Kurt left the second man to introduce himself.

"Mako Storm, at your service."

"Cut out the James Bond act, Mako," Alicia scolded him. She turned to me. "He's an associate, feel free to ignore him. How'd the diving lessons go?"

TJ shrugged.

"I was hoping for someone more to my liking for the buddy breathing thing," Mako said, miming an hourglass shape with his hands.

"Whatcha got, babe?" TJ went over to Alicia's desk and kissed the top of her head, then sat down in the captain's chair.

All eyes turned to me. I told an abbreviated version of my story.

"Got it. What do we have?" TJ asked, scanning the screens. He pulled a keyboard over the arm of the chair.

"Sandoval Cartel, with an interesting tie to the Little Palm Island Resort."

"That's Mac Travis' neck of the woods," TJ said.

"I thought of that, but let's see if we can pin this down. If Harvey's daughter and Mendoza are heading south, the resort seems like a logical place."

"No shit," Mako said, studying his phone. "Check this out: A best-kept secret for US presidents and celebrities, Little Palm Island Resort and Spa is located off the fabled Florida Keys coastline, on a lush, private island dotted with crushed seashell paths amid verdant tropical foliage. Each of the fifteen redesigned thatched-roof bunga-lows offers—"

Alicia cut him off. "We don't need the brochure."

"I volunteer to check it out," Mako said.

"Not for two grand a night, you're not," Alicia said.

"Those kind of rates'll ensure privacy." TJ pecked at his keyboard.

The last group of monitors lit up, showing a satellite view of the resort. It really was an oasis among other barren islands.

"Right on the Atlantic. Easy in and out. You can see anyone coming for miles. Deep-water marina too. Makes sense. Let me see if I can get into their security system."

"You do that. I'm going to call Mac," Alicia said.

I moved next to Kurt. "Who's this Mac guy?"

"He might be the guy to help finish this off, but you'd never guess it from looking at him."

"I've learned not to make any judgments after this past week."

"Haven't seen him in a couple of years, but he and his girlfriend, Mel, are good people. Finding him might be a problem, though."

"What do you mean?"

"They live on an island about ten miles into the Gulf."

"Had to leave a message," Alicia said. "I'll email Mel, probably have better luck that way."

Mako left the room. TJ was still working when he returned with a large drink with a lime. He had a can of regular Coke, which he handed to TJ, and a Diet Coke, which he gave to Alicia.

"Guess I've been reduced to a waiter. Get you anything?" he asked Kurt and me.

We both shook our heads and watched TJ. He cracked the tab on the can and took a long sip, then set it down and smiled.

"Gotcha."

Rico Mendoza's picture and bio disappeared and were replaced by several views of what appeared to be a resort. A minute later each screen showed a different camera, with one on the dock. The flamered Baja was partially hidden behind a large cabin cruiser.

"That's Mendoza's boat!"

TJ and Alicia turned to me.

"Easy, Harvey. Good to know we're onto them."

"Can you see if they're aboard?" Alicia asked.

"Can't manipulate the cameras remotely, but if we're patient we could get lucky."

The wait was interrupted by Alicia's phone. It was Mac Travis, and she started to explain what was happening.

"Can you put him on speaker? I'd rather plead my case directly."

A second later I heard a whoosh of wind. "This is Harvey Thackerson."

"Travis here."

"Thank you for calling back. I'm afraid your friends have put your name forward. I wanted to explain myself." The only sound on the other end of the line while I told the story was the wind. He must have been on a boat.

"My mate and I are up your way. I can be there in an hour."

"Thank you."

Another voice broke through. "Y'all got any beer or do we need to stop?"

"Tru!" Alicia exclaimed. "We got you covered."

It was by far the most emotion I had seen from her.

The most unlikely people had helped me over the last week, and I recalled my promise not to judge. With an hour to wait and maybe more if nothing appeared on the screen to confirm that Mendoza and Victoria were on the island, I started to fidget.

"Come on, man, Mako'll give you something for your nerves."

"It'll be late by the time I get back. I should probably say good-bye," Kurt said. He hugged Alicia and TJ and headed out of the war room. We said goodbye in the kitchen, and I thanked him again.

"Let me know how it turns out," he said and left.

"So, Harvey, what'll you have?"

"I'd better keep a clear head."

"You sound like my father." Mako scrounged through the liquor cabinet like it was his. He came out with a bottle of rum and proceeded to mix a drink with some other liquor and orange juice from the refrigerator. "Painkiller. It'll cure what ails you."

He handed me the drink, and I took a sip so as not to be rude. "That's not bad." The concoction did as advertised and calmed my nerves, but it also knocked me off my feet. I moved to the couch and sat down, realizing I was still exhausted. My head fell back against the cushion.

"Yo, yo, yo, Alicia baby."

I woke up with a start. For a brief second, I thought I might be dreaming, until I saw the tall man peering at me over the back of the couch. His hair dangled around his face.

"You Harvey? I'm Tru. This here's Mac."

I'd forgotten about the man on the phone asking for beer. It took a second to shake the cobwebs from my head. Once it was clear, I rose and shook their hands. "That's me. Thank you for coming down."

"Actually it's up, but no worries," Trufante said.

"Don't mind him. He is what he is," Mac said.

A few seconds later Alicia appeared. She almost ran to Trufante and threw her arms around him.

"Easy there, girl." He turned to me. "Girlfriend and I have shared a few adventures."

I shrugged.

"Where's that beer at, girl? Ole Mac's been working me hard."

"Hardly. We've been down off Islamorada checking some spots. I do the work, he drives the boat."

"Hey! I might have something," TJ called from the war room.

A few seconds later we were gathered around the captain's chair. TJ slid one of the video feeds over to cover several of the middle screens.

"That's her!" For a second I thought Victoria was alone. Then Mendoza walked into the picture. The camera angle was designed to watch several cabanas on the beach.

Victoria and Mendoza were arguing. There was no sound and the view was too distant to make an attempt at lip reading, but their body language was self-explanatory. Mendoza made a move toward her with an open hand, but she backed out of his reach.

I still had no idea which end of the game she was playing, and the action on the screen told me little. It could as easily be construed as a lovers' quarrel as a struggle between two adversaries. I leaned toward the former. If it were the latter, she would probably be dead soon.

"You know her. What do you think?" Mac asked me.

"Guy's a jerk," Trufante said, crumbling the beer can. He left the room to get another.

"Nothing like a fiery Latina," Mako said.

I was about to say something, but Alicia handled him. "Why don't you keep an eye on the Cajun?"

Mako put his head down, muttered something about being reduced to a babysitter, and left the room, leaving me with Mac, Alicia, and TJ. On-screen, Mendoza said something to Victoria and turned away. Victoria looked directly at the camera. Her hands were open, palm out in her lap. With her right hand, she placed her thumbs inside her palm and closed her hand, then repeated the gesture.

"What's that?" I asked.

"She must have seen the camera. The hand signal is a call for help."

I was relieved to know that she hadn't joined the cartel, but now we had to get there to save her. "Can you take me down there, Mac?"

"I'll do one better. We'll help you get her back."

26

SHAMELESS
STEVEN BECKER

CHASING VICTORIA and Rico Mendoza made me feel like I was drowning. Every time I thought we were going to catch them, something happened and they escaped. I was worn out, but at the same time, I felt alive. In the past week, thanks to Kate and Tony, I had relearned to shoot. My boat skills had also improved, making me wonder how I had ever managed to single-handedly drive the O'Day from Boston to the Keys.

My body was battered, but my confidence had grown. Perseverance was an attribute I understood. Somewhere deep inside, I knew if I kept my faith and fought through the obstacles in my way that we would catch Mendoza.

At least I understood Victoria's motivation now. Getting her back might help with the sting of learning that Martha may have been murdered by the cartel as well. My wife and I had come through the dark teenage years. Victoria had always been headstrong. Surviving what she had as a young teen ingrained that into a person. I'd got some of that in the Navy.

Hit the wall, get over the wall, keep going.

Mac Travis had perseverance running through his veins. He was one of those guys who didn't say much, but when he did, you listened.

As we cruised southwest aboard Mac's boat, the *Tin Can*, I watched the screen showing our position and course relative to the Keys. The manufacturer of the chartplotter was the same as the one I had been forced to learn on the O'Day. I understood the unit better than my cellphone—the one that I had tossed into the Gulf out by Shark Key.

The boat was utilitarian. Made from aluminum—hence its name —it featured a drop-down bow similar to a World War II landing craft. The catamaran hull design with the twin 300 HP engines shot the boat through the water. The two-foot waves were no obstacle.

We were past the Seven Mile Bridge, running a course about a mile offshore in Hawks Channel that paralleled the islands. The route was similar to the one I had taken on my trip down. The Intra-coastal Waterway runs on the Gulf side, but I had chosen the Atlantic side for the ease of navigation.

The old trestle bridge across the Bahia Honda Channel was the next landmark. Once past that iconic bridge, we would be about four miles from the Little Palm Island Resort. I only hoped we would reach it in time.

"We're going to pull up outside the channel," Mac yelled over the engine noise.

We were traveling along a string of barrier islands. Mac stopped about a quarter mile short of the red marker outside the channel.

"Can you handle the boat?" he asked.

I glanced over at Trufante, who seemed more interested in his next beer than in getting my daughter back.

"Don't mind him. When we need him, he'll be there."

I shrugged and moved to the helm.

There was no comparison between the *Tin Can* and the O'Day, but I'd been watching Mac work for a while. The twin engines were a concern, though.

Mac walked out of the wheelhouse and moved forward, where he opened a hatch and pulled out a mesh bag with dive gear. He brought it to the rear cockpit and removed a pair of long fins, a mask, and a snorkel.

"You're going to drop me over there," he said, pointing to a large island. "Just past where all the palm trees are is the resort. I'm going to swim over and have a look."

"What do you want me to do?"

"Any luck, I'll be back in thirty minutes. If not, get the Cajun to call Pip. He should be here shortly."

Mac held his mask over the side and wet it, then spat in it and rinsed it with seawater. He pulled it over his head and placed it backward on his forehead while he put his fins on. Once he was ready, he slid the mask around, checked the seal, placed the snorkel into his mouth, and nodded to me. I returned the gesture.

Mac slid into the water like an eel and disappeared. I knew where he was going and watched the tip of the snorkel where it pierced the surface, leaving a small wake behind him. A few minutes later he reached the beach and sat backward while he removed his fins. He stashed them and the mask by a small bush and moved toward the interior of the island.

Once I had seen the Baja at the dock, I had studied the satellite images and the resort's website. The island was the last in a string of barrier islands that enclosed a lagoon. It was a green oasis in the middle of paradise. Just about all of the islands were covered in mangroves. Some had small beaches, while on others only the brush covered their shorelines. On some of the dryer land areas the trees were mostly dead, victims of Hurricane Irma's storm surge. It made me wonder if mangroves were the cockroaches of the tropical flora world.

I'd seen the price tags for the resort's rooms and agreed with Alicia that there were only three kinds of people who would pay that much. One was the corporate kingpins, who wrote it off as a business expense. Then came the jet-setters, whose yachts were docked by the resort and were more luxurious than any house I'd ever furnished through my store—and were left empty as their owners stayed ashore.

The last were the guys who paid cash and didn't care how much anything cost because the money was from ill-gotten gains.

The resort was the perfect investment for the cartel, as a place to hole up or as a near-perfect setting for a clandestine meeting. Either use suited Mendoza.

I continued to watch the resort, but there was no sign of Mac. He'd been gone for about fifteen minutes. In that time the *Tin Can* had drifted a fair distance. I was moving to the helm to reposition it when I saw a boat coming directly toward us.

This was too much like deja vu, but this time I knew what to do. I reached up and pulled the shotgun from the racks on the ceiling and checked the chamber. It was empty, so I chambered a round, set the weapon on the seat next to me, and pressed the throttles forward.

Trufante jumped up like a cat and stood beside me. "You got this?"

Not trusting him, I nodded. Mac said he'd be there if I needed him, but my gut told me not to rely on him.

I'd watched Chase, Kurt Hunter, and Mac run fast boats, but was still surprised at the speed with which the *Tin Can* shot forward. I backed off the throttles quickly and started to steer back to the area where I had dropped Mac. The approaching boat mirrored my movement.

Too many people had stood in front of me this past week, and some had paid for it. I was determined not to be a victim again and picked up the shotgun.

"Easy there, hoss." Trufante placed a lean hand on the barrel and brought it down.

I brushed him off and moved to the starboard gunwale facing the ocean side, placed the stock firmly against my shoulder, and raised the barrel. The boat continued on its collision course. I took a breath and fired, then chambered another round.

The Cajun jerked the shotgun from my grasp. "Tryin' to tell you, he's a friendly."

The boat had slowed but continued its approach. I was mad at

Trufante, but something told me the cartoonish figure behind the wheel of the approaching boat was here to help. The driver was short and stocky with a red, white, and blue bandanna over what looked like a shaved head. The butt of a cold cigar was clamped in his mouth.

"Yo, Tru, what's up with that shit?" the driver called out as he coasted to a stop.

The bow wake reached the *Tin Can*, forcing me to hold on.

The man glanced at me. "Who the hell are you?" he called out. "Where's Travis?"

"I'm Harvey—"

Trufante jumped in. "Old folks here is a little jumpy. Mac went ashore to check things out. Left me to keep an eye on him." He turned to me. "This here's Pip."

I clenched my fists.

"Nice job, you piece of Bayou trash. Son of a bitch almost shot me," Pip said, his expression unreadable.

I turned to Trufante to see what his reaction would be. A grin as wide as the grill of my old Cadillac greeted me.

The tension dropped, and Pip clicked a lighter that was more of a flame thrower. He disappeared in a cloud of smoke.

"Y'all don't need to worry about Pip here. He likes to make an entrance." Trufante reached his long arms out and lassoed the aft cleat with a dock line. He pulled the boats together.

"Where's Travis?" Pip asked between puffs. "Boy needs watching, if you know what I mean."

I glanced at my watch and saw the thirty minutes had almost expired. "Should be back around now."

"If that gunshot didn't get him caught."

"I got that message," I said.

"Well anyways, we're here to help. Heard the cartel has your daughter."

"Something like that." That simplified things.

"Mac said to call you if he wasn't back in thirty minutes." I glanced at my watch. "It's just past that." My confidence in his backup wasn't high, but if Mac trusted them, I would too. I also had no choice.

"So, here's the thing." Pip paused and puffed. "We wait. Travis ain't done anything on time in his life."

I wasn't sure that was the best tactic and started to say something when a loud engine cut through my words. I glanced around, wondering what it was. I'd been in and around all kinds of boats in the past week and it didn't sound like any of them.

"Seaplane," Trufante said once the volume leveled out.

"Boy's right. Follow me," Pip said.

Trufante released the line. Pip waited a long second for the current to separate the boats, then pushed down the throttles and moved away. I did the same, trying to follow his wake so I didn't have to deal with the large waves, one of the many things I had learned on my sail south.

He was headed out to sea. I turned back to look at the resort, hoping to see Mac on the beach, but he wasn't there. Just as I started to wonder if I shouldn't have a Plan C, Pip swung the boat around the channel marker and headed toward the resort.

I started to follow but saw a line of signs indicating shallow water. Brown, brown, run aground, was another lesson remembered from my sail, and the water in front of me was brown. Our two boats were almost parallel now, but facing opposite directions. Trufante made a hand motion indicating I should go around the outside of the marker. I didn't want to waste the time, but there was no choice.

Over the whine of the outboards, I heard the sound of the seaplane's engine start to rev up. Somehow I knew it had something to do with Victoria.

I lost my footing for a second as I cut the wheel too hard around the piling, barely avoiding another injury. The boat righted itself and me with it, as I corrected course to follow Pip.

I could see the front of the resort. A long dock extended into the water, with the large yacht we'd seen on the surveillance footage secured to it. The Baja remained behind it. Just past it, I saw the seaplane as it taxied away from the dock.

Pip had slowed to an idle just past the seaplane. Trufante was turned to the dock, where I saw a man waving. A second look told me it was Mac, and he was waving at me.

Docking the boat was over my skill level, and I wondered if I should lower the bow platform. I decided that would take too much time. I had no choice but to suck it up. The only thing in my favor was the boat. Unlike the shiny fiberglass models around me, it was aluminum and showed the scars of a workboat. Adding another ding was not an issue.

I'd avoided docks like the plague with the sailboat, but I knew a few things. The first was that if you are going to hit, hit slow. I gently pushed the throttles forward and cut a wide arc that I hoped would land me next to the dock.

The boat stopped several feet shy of the dock, and I was about to give the throttles another nudge when something struck the outside of the wheelhouse. Before I could react, Mac jumped aboard. He moved directly to the helm which I gladly surrendered.

"The seaplane. They've got her."

27

SHAMELESS
STEVEN BECKER

MAC FOLLOWED Pip in the direction the seaplane had taken. The pilot was taxiing across a wide harbor. The day of the week had meant nothing since the chase had started. Now, looking around the water I had to guess it was a weekend.

I'd considered Newfound Harbor as an overnight anchorage on the way down. Instead of dealing with questionable holding for the anchor, something I'd learned a lot about over the trip, I recalled there was a single, deep channel with shoals and small islands scattered throughout the harbor. Instead of worrying about the navigation, I'd chosen to stop for the night at one of the mooring balls that marked some snorkeling spots on the outside of the barrier islands on the way down.

The seaplane was heading west, directly across the waterway and away from the resort. I figured the pilot needed to create a runway of sorts to take off into the east wind, or at least that's what I remembered about planes. With its pontoons barely drawing any water, the pilot was able to use a direct course to his imaginary starting point where Pip and Mac were forced to skirt the shoals. I thought that might work to our advantage as it wouldn't appear that we were following them.

"How can we stop a plane?"

"He can't take off without clear water. The lookie-loos will help with that."

I glanced ahead and saw a large group of boats in front of a small island. A large houseboat flying numerous flags seemed to anchor the party.

"Picnic Island. Local sandbar," Mac said.

Before I could ask how he intended to involve the locals, I watched as several boats pulled anchor or lifted the anchoring poles mounted to their transoms and started to shadow the plane.

Phones were out, with several people on each craft taking pictures. The pilot continued as if they weren't there, suddenly turning 180 degrees. The boats turned with him and waited as he ran up his engines. The plane lurched forward slowly building speed with the boats following on either side, but not interfering with the plane's progress.

"Pip ain't gonna risk his boat. It'll be up to us." Mac glanced at me. "Get ready with the shotgun. We get even with them, I want you to pump as many shots into the engine as you can. If you hit the propeller that probably wouldn't hurt, either."

I reached for the gun and moved out of the wheelhouse. Kneeling down at the portside, I braced my elbows on the flat part of the gunwale and started to track the plane with the barrel.

Mac was just behind and to the side of the plane. Two other boats were directly in front of him following the same course. Each boat accelerated to match the increasing speed of the plane as it prepared to take off.

What I didn't know was how fast the plane needed to go. What I did know was that it was up to me to stop it. As I followed the plane with the sights, my biggest fear was that I would miss and hit Victoria. Aiming ahead of the plane, a sudden acceleration would shift the shot toward the fuselage. Fortunately, we were on the plane's portside, so a stray shot would likely hit the pilot.

A stream of boats accompanied the plane, but none hindered its progress. That was, until Pip's boat flashed across its path. There was little risk to it, but he did force the pilot to slow. He wove back and forth several times. The tactic should have worked—except for a shoal directly in his path. The plane skimmed over it, but Pip was forced to stop.

"Up to you, Harvey," Mac called back.

When I left the Navy I thought I'd never fire a gun again, especially not in anger, and with my daughter at risk of a stray shot. My hands trembled, making the gun shift, then I realized that Mac had crossed a wake and cut inside the other boats. He was right. If I was going to do something it needed to be done now.

"Count of ten," Mac called.

Trufante was by my side, his long arm pointing at the plane. "Right there, my man."

The boat shot forward as I counted down in my head. When I reached four, we were even with the plane. I didn't wait any longer and fired, chambered another round, and fired again. A stream of smoke appeared from the plane's cowling, but its engine didn't seem affected. I could tell from the tone as it roared beside us, much louder than Mac's outboard engines.

There was nothing else I could do but watch as streams of water trailed from the pontoons as they broke the surface tension of the water. An inch at a time, the plane ascended above the surface.

Mac was forced to slow by the same obstacle that had hindered Pip. I moved to the wheelhouse for a better look at the plane taking my daughter away from me.

Boats were one thing. We'd had enough trouble tracking Mendoza's progress over the water. In the air, it was altogether impossible.

"I think you hit something," Trufante called out from the bow.

I couldn't see anything.

"Boy knows his engines," Mac said as he accelerated around the shoal. I grabbed the seat for balance as the lightweight hull rocked back and forth. My brain focused on staying erect, and at first, I missed the change in tone from the plane's engine. I hauled myself to my full height and watched as it struggled to grab air and failed.

The port pontoon hit first, and for a long second the fuselage seemed to titter on the brink of taking the plane over. That would be as much of a danger to Victoria as a gunshot. The water was crystal clear, and I could see the seagrass on the bottom flattened out by the tide. The visibility was deceiving. A glance at the chartplotter showed we were in five feet of water—not enough for Victoria to drown if she were standing, but upside down in the cockpit, she could easily be trapped.

It appeared the plane was regaining its equilibrium when the pontoon struck something. Suddenly the momentum swung the other way. Sometimes these kinds of things happen in slow motion. That wasn't the case now as the plane violently pitchpoled.

Just what I feared—the plane settled upside down and sat on the bottom with the pontoons facing the sky.

Mac wasted no time and sped toward the wreck. "Take the wheel, Harvey."

I didn't question him. Mac moved away from the helm. I took his place and tentatively steered toward the plane.

We were the first boat on scene, with Pip a few seconds behind. The rest of the fleet that had been following the plane settled around us with their phones held high, more interested in taking pictures and videos than assisting.

Mac took a quick look around and dove into the shallow water. He reached the plane, gulped a deep breath, and descended. I could see him in the clear water as he swam down one side of the plane, surfaced, and checked the other side. Stopping at where the hatch would be, he took another breath and descended again. Bubbles shot to the surface as he appeared to fight the locking mechanism.

Watching Mac, I didn't notice that Trufante had moved next to me.

"Might have to get wet." He pulled his T-shirt over his head and stepped toward the gunwale.

"You need a crowbar or something? The hatch must be jammed."

Trufante turned away from the water. "Try the holds by the transom, I'll check the wheelhouse."

We both started searching through the holds, but found nothing suitable.

"Come on man, anything."

The only thing I saw was the shotgun. I held it up and the Cajun nodded. He grabbed it and slid over the side. Within a few seconds, he was beside Mac at the fuselage. Mac stepped back and Trufante slammed the stock into the door mechanism. By the time he made his fourth attempt, they had company. A handful of other men from nearby boats had put down their phones and joined them.

Chaos ensued, but Mac and Trufante held their position. Several boats nudged closer, some trying to help, others trying to take pictures. It was a dangerous situation. I was surprised there was no law enforcement or first responders arriving. The only semi-official vessel was a beautiful wooden boat called the *Woodson* that served as the shuttle from the mainland to the resort.

Two men hopped over its gunwale and waded to the wreck. They moved with authority, holding their pistols at the high-ready position, just out of the water. Boats started to back away, and some of the people trying to assist with the rescue dispersed.

Mac and Trufante were oblivious to the situation. Their sole focus was on the door. Trufante wound up and swung again, this time with some result. The door swung sideways toward the front of the plane. Water rushed into the fuselage. Seconds later, several figures were visible in the opening.

Rico Mendoza pushed Victoria down the short ladder to the pontoon. With a pistol in each hand, both pointed at Victoria, he followed. I took a deep breath, relieved to see that she was alright. Trufante swung the shotgun to use in its intended purpose, but he was too late. The men from the *Woodson* grabbed him and took the gun.

The wooden boat started to back toward the seaplane. With no regard for the gleaming finish, the captain nudged up against the pontoon. Mendoza stepped into the boat and held his hand out for Victoria. I had a misplaced proud dad moment as she shook it off and followed him aboard.

The two men prodded Trufante toward the *Woodson*. I caught Victoria's eye and saw a pleading look. One that would stay with me to my grave. I was steeled for action but had no weapon. My only option seemed to be the oldest naval trick in the book—ram the other boat. I moved to the wheelhouse and was about to push down on the throttles when Mac appeared beside me.

"The smart move is to get out of here and make a plan." He pointed toward the north. "Head for the bridge."

I knew it was the right course of action. The plane was disabled, and at the least, we would be able to track the resort shuttle. The only problem now was we had to rescue Trufante as well as Victoria.

The *Woodson* started to move off in the direction of the resort. It was not a good feeling to head in the opposite direction, although it was the logical one.

I glanced back after crossing through the ragged opening in the old railway bridge and then under the span across the highway to see Pip behind us.

We both slowed. "We're not much worse off," Mac said, as I pulled up alongside Pip's boat. "Trufante can take care of her now."

I pursed my lips, trying not to express my feelings. Once again in my quest to save my daughter I had put an innocent in danger.

"What are we going to do?"

"Get help," Mac said.

I shrugged and went back inside the wheelhouse. Pip took off, heading for a neighborhood on Big Pine Key. I followed and slowed just after he did as we entered a narrow canal system.

My mind was busy trying to memorize the half-dozen turns we took in case I had to replicate the route myself. About ten minutes later, Pip stopped just off a concrete seawall. Mac put out a couple of fenders and told me to close the gap. When the boat was within a few feet, Mac stepped across the void with a line in his hand. He secured the boat and went to help Pip.

I eased the boat in and was startled by a loud pop. A few seconds later a young woman emerged from underneath the stilt house carrying a dead iguana by the tail.

"Harvey, this is Pamela. She's good help in these kinds of situations."

28

SHAMELESS
STEVEN BECKER

THE WOMAN DROPPED the iguana into a chest freezer set against the wall of a storage enclosure. With the rifle pointed at the ground, she reached into the pocket of her cutoff jeans and removed a cigarette, which she lit with a lighter. It looked like it was hand-rolled, which was soon confirmed by the distinctive smell.

She walked over to me and extended the joint. "You look distressed, this ought to help."

I declined. The woman struck me as an enigma. She was tall—though several inches shorter than Trufante—and maybe about Mac's height. Like the Cajun and Mac, she was lean and muscular, a physique earned through real life, not the gym. She had a hippy kind of look that didn't quite mesh with her Annie Oakley act.

"Damned iguanas." She stepped to the side, lifted the air rifle, and popped another one of the reptiles from two dozen feet. "They're eating my hibiscus." She looked around before setting off to retrieve the kill. "Where's Tru?"

"He's in trouble and Harvey needs some help." Mac explained the situation.

"What're we doing sitting here shooting iguanas, then?" She

dropped the creature in the freezer and headed up the outside stairs that serviced the stilt house.

I glanced over to see Pip emerge from a cloud of cigar smoke with a beer. Mac was still sober, but I wondered about this crew. My fears were somewhat assuaged when Pamela returned carrying a handgun and a rifle with a scope. She had pulled on a water-colored, long-sleeved camo fishing shirt over her bikini top.

The group gathered around the *Tin Can*.

"What are we up against?" Pamela asked.

"We've seen three men, all armed. And Harvey's daughter. Assume she's a good guy."

"Guy driving the boat had to be one of them, too. Might have the captain as a hostage," Pip said.

"Interesting. Transportation?"

"Looks like they hijacked the *Woodson*. They headed in the direction of the resort, but they could have gone anywhere."

She glanced at Pip's stripped-down boat. "I thought y'all were working on that."

I followed her gaze. The boat looked good from a distance but a closer examination showed everything that could be removed, had. That included three massive holes in the dashboard where the electronics had been.

"These things take time. Found the sons of bitches though, didn't we."

"Been more beer drinking than working, if I know you and Tru."

Pip turned a shade of red which he tried to hide behind a cloud of smoke. "Boy's got skills." He pulled a nickel-plated revolver from a compartment in the dash.

"What are you gonna do with that?" Pamela asked.

"THAT is all I need."

"I got THAT and raise you eleven." She held up her pistol, the extended magazine adding another inch to the butt.

"Y'all done?" Mac asked and stepped aboard the *Tin Can*. I followed him with Pamela and Pip behind me. We were underway a few minutes later.

"Pip, take the wheel."

I had to admit I was relieved to be a spectator for a while.

Pip started to navigate the canal system. Mac picked up his phone. "I'm going to call Mel and see if she can pull up the signal from the AIS transponder on the *Woodson*. They probably haven't thought to disable it."

Just as we were about to exit the canal system, Mel called back. Mac asked her to check if the seaplane had filed a flight plan, and disconnected.

She called back a few minutes later. "They're headed to Marathon. My guess is the airport there."

Pip had just passed the last of three akimbo PVC pipes marking the channel.

He looked over at Mac. "Where to?"

"Marathon. Probably the airport."

"Makes sense. My boat would have been faster."

"Running blind into a gunfight with your six-shooter your idea of smart?"

"Point, Travis. I'm working on it."

Pip pressed the throttles down. We were quickly under the bridge, retracing the route we had taken from Marathon earlier, though this time Pip stayed much closer to land. He switched his left-hand display to radar, and we crowded around the helm as the screen populated.

"Too much clutter. Gotta get into open water," Mac said.

We were about a quarter mile from the resort. "Baja's still there, they must be aboard that old boat."

"That old boat is only six years old. Wood veneer over fiberglass."

That meant it was probably fast, too. We rounded the marker and headed east. The radar screen cleared somewhat now that we had open water ahead. It was easy to place the boats tied to the mooring balls. Beyond that were several returns.

I felt helpless, with nothing to do for the time being except to watch the screen refresh. Slowly I noticed a trend, with a single boat moving on the same course we were. The rings on the screen were at two-mile intervals with the return in the third one. That meant they were between four and six miles ahead.

Mel called several times with updates from her tracking software. So far, Mac seemed to be correct. My worry now was speed. Pip answered that question by pressing the throttles to the stop and trimming the engines. I appreciated his sense of urgency.

I knew from my two previous trips along the coast that Marathon was twenty-odd miles from the resort. It was a large area, though. Often mistaken for a single key, the City of Marathon was actually comprised of several islands, Vaca Key being the largest. Vaca Cut on the eastern end, Sister Creek near the middle, and Boot Creek Harbor were the three main channels used to reach the Atlantic. A handful of private channels cut through the flats and extended from some of the canals as well. The Gulf side was accessible by water along most of its length.

"They're going under the bridge," I said, watching the blip on the screen.

"We need a better route." Mac glanced at the screen. "If the airport is the destination, I have a pretty good idea where they're headed."

As we approached Marathon, the landmass cluttered the radar screen to the point where a single vessel was indistinguishable.

I turned my attention to the water ahead. Mac shut down the radar and switched the screen to another, zoomed-in view of the chartplotter. He panned to the airport and placed his finger at the end of a small rectangular body of water adjacent to the runway.

"Aviation Boulevard boat ramp. That's where I'd go."

There appeared to be a single route to the ramp, which would mean we'd arrive well behind the other boats. A well-coordinated pickup could have Victoria in the air before we reached the runway.

He panned the screen to show the Atlantic side. "Eighty-sixth Street hits a vacant lot that goes right to the highway." He traced the line of the canal adjacent to the road. The island was skinny here, mostly taken by the airport and US 1. The canal ended in a T where they would be able to leave the boat. They would have to cross US 1 to reach the airport, but it looked like the faster route.

Pip continued straight past a couple of smaller keys and shot across a string of day beacons instead of turning into the channel. Two-thirds of the way along the Seven Mile Bridge was Moser Channel. The bridge's sixty-five-foot clearance, one of only a handful of places in the Keys that a sailboat can cross from the Atlantic to the Gulf, lay ahead. We all glanced under the span hoping to see the *Woodson*.

Mac and Pip continued to discuss the course. I turned to see Pamela field-stripping the rifle and set aside my first opinion. I'd watched Marines do the same before any action, including range drills.

We passed Boot Key and the entrance to Sister Creek, then Sombrero Beach. Pip changed course and steered to the outside of a single island labeled East Sister Rock. The "rock" was developed as an estate. Once we were clear of the shoal surrounding the island, he cut the wheel to port and headed directly for the narrow channel.

We passed several similar cuts all marked with a collection of PVC pipes. Pip took a hard turn into the channel at speed, then slowed once we reached the actual canal.

"Port side, Travis," he called out.

Mac moved quickly. He had two fenders out and over the side in a matter of seconds. "Get a line for the stern," he called to me as Mac looped one through and then around the bow cleat.

I found the line and did what he asked. Once my line was secure, I glanced up to see that Pip was coming in hot. I thought he was going to crash when he suddenly cut the wheel and dropped the port motor into full reverse. The boat settled against the seawall.

Mac was over the gunwale with his line. I followed with mine. Pip shut down the engines and grabbed his revolver.

We stood on the seawall for a long second. Mac turned to me. "We're a little light on weapons since they took the shotgun. Maybe it'd be better if you stayed with the boat."

"She's my girl. I'm going."

We took off as a group across the empty lot and reached US 1. This was one of the few four-lane sections of the Overseas Highway, making it difficult to cross. There was finally a break in the traffic that got us to the median. As we waited to cross the far lanes, I noticed a small plane coming in from the west.

Like the seaplane, it needed to take off and land into the wind, which meant the plane would be taking off from the west end of the runway. Mac must have had the same thought as we crossed to the access road. The airport terminal was deserted, with only a few charter outfits and a car rental. As we ran through the terminal I wondered how we were going to get through security.

We had made it to the tarmac without incident when I realized that there were no commercial carriers here, hence no security. The relief was short-lived when I spotted four figures running across the runway. Victoria was easy to recognize, as was Rico Mendoza. The other men looked like the guys from the *Woodson*. Trufante was noticeably absent.

"That them, Mac Travis?" Pamela asked.

"Yeah. The one behind the woman is the leader."

"Head of the snake." She took off at a run toward a line of heavy trucks. At least one displayed the hazardous placard for fuel.

The plane I had seen coming in when we crossed the highway was taxiing toward the fuel truck. My initial fear was that the pilot would land and pick up the passengers on the run, but it appeared he needed fuel. In my long string of near misses and bad luck, this was the first break I'd had.

Mac directed Pip to the other side of the maintenance area. "Harvey, stay with me."

He led me to a short concrete wall surrounding the trucks. We watched as the driver positioned the vehicle to within a dozen feet of where the plane stopped. He stepped out of the cab and moved to the rear of the truck, where he started to uncoil the fuel hose.

Mac glanced at me. "Take the truck."

It made sense. The driver had probably left the keys in the ignition, and no fuel meant no flight. I took a deep breath and started to walk casually around the enclosure until I reached two open, chain-link gates. I entered the area like I belonged and walked directly to the truck.

The driver was on the other side, dragging the hose toward the plane when I got in the cab. A quick glance showed the keys in the ignition. I took another breath and turned the key. The engine started and I dropped the transmission into drive. Without waiting, I pulled out of the enclosure and headed down the access road beside the runway, dragging the hose behind me.

A glance in the rearview mirror showed the driver standing stunned as the hose was torn out of his hands. He yelled at me but I ignored him, more worried about the three men approaching from the other side.

The area was wide open, but I felt safe inside the fuel truck. It wasn't a likely target for gunfire. My confidence was misplaced, though, as a shot was fired my way.

29

SHAMELESS
STEVEN BECKER

I DROVE to the other side of the runway and waited. With the window down, I heard a conversation in Spanish from across the way. It sounded like Mendoza was ordering his men to take the truck. I didn't have to wait long for confirmation, as the men came across the runway.

Moving the truck made sense. It had at least delayed the flight. I was still unsure of Victoria's motives, though. She had told me clearly to stay away from her back in Palm Beach, but then flashed the distress sign in the resort. There had been a quick glance before Mendoza took her in the Baja. El Tigre had reassured me that she was innocent, but I wasn't about to trust that woman. Those few moments held the only communication we'd had, and it could be interpreted several ways.

Mendoza held his gun at his side. From his body language, I suspected he didn't totally trust Victoria, either. That gave me some hope, but it also made our position more difficult. Mac and company couldn't fire on Mendoza without risking a bullet striking Victoria.

The men were halfway across the runway. I had two options— either try and take them out with the truck, which would risk an all-out gun battle, or abandon ship.

I chose the latter, taking the keys with me.

I slid across the seat and exited the vehicle through the passenger door, then moved back to the rear of the truck. I peered around the tank and saw the men split up as if they planned on just driving the truck across the tarmac. The position of their weapons, held high and ready, told me I had made a correct decision.

They moved toward the front of the truck and I waited until the man heading for the passenger door was out of sight before I ran. Ignoring my aching knee, I sprinted toward the tall grass beside the runway. I reached the brush and rolled into the weeds.

Two doors slammed closed almost simultaneously, telling me I hadn't been observed. I recognized the Spanish word *llaves* as they searched the cab for the keys. While I waited for them to give up, I studied Victoria and Mendoza, trying to determine how to handle them.

The men gave up a minute later. They left the truck and hurried back across the runway. I glanced over at the truck and then at Victoria, wondering if she would remember her driving lessons as a teenager.

We'd had fight after fight, mostly with me trying to tame her aggressiveness behind the wheel. There had been one final incident that caused me to finally give up and pass the baton to a driving instructor. If she remembered, it would tell me her intentions and at the same time give me a chance to free her.

I waited and watched the men for a long second to make sure they didn't turn back. When they reached the other end of the runway I made my move. Taking the keys from my pocket, I ran to the truck, opened the passenger door, and climbed in. I slid across the seat and jammed the key into the ignition.

I paused after the truck started to see if anyone had noticed. The cartel men were still a couple of hundred feet from Mendoza and Victoria when I shifted into drive and gunned the engine.

They hadn't heard the engine start, but all eyes were on the truck as I sped across the runway, heading directly for Mendoza and Victoria. My intention was to separate the men from Mendoza, allowing Mac to take them while I went for Victoria.

As I continued to accelerate the truck started to vibrate. Confined to the airport, it probably hadn't run at this speed in years, which also meant the brakes hadn't ever been stood on, either. The speedometer told me I was approaching seventy. It was too late to worry about Mac's reaction. I was committed.

Over the roar of the truck, gunshots rang out. I couldn't risk looking at who was shooting at whom, only hope it wasn't at me. My focus was on Mendoza and Victoria. From a couple of hundred feet away, I saw them turn toward me.

At about a hundred feet away, Mendoza would have no doubt of my intentions.

Victoria had been a headstrong teenager and had gotten some kind of thrill from playing chicken. It was probably from watching my distress at her actions rather than the thrill of the game. As these things often do, a family joke had come of it. "Never give in. Wavering is for chickens." Life lessons came from unlikely places.

Mendoza raised his gun and I ducked, braking hard and fighting to hold the wheel straight. The windshield shattered as a bullet struck the tempered glass. I held a death grip on the wheel, knowing if I faltered it could cost Victoria her life.

I wished I could have looked into her eyes when she understood, but I was holding on for dear life.

A game of chicken offers several outcomes. Mutual destruction is one, but it's more usual for one party to flinch. Ego often dictated who that would be. I was counting on Rico Mendoza seeing an old man behind the wheel and figuring I wouldn't go through with it. He would underestimate me and stand his ground.

I could only hope Victoria knew it wasn't going to be me who flinched.

The gap closed faster than I expected. At the last second, Victoria dove away from Mendoza, and in his moment of indecision, I ran him over.

There was no time to check on him or Victoria. I had my work cut out for me if I was to save myself. The walled enclosure was on my left and the plane on my right, leaving me no choice but to go straight. My right foot had moved from the gas pedal to the brakes the second I heard the thump, causing the truck to fishtail to the right, grazing the concrete wall of the enclosure. I jerked the wheel to the left trying to avoid a crash and eased up slightly on the brake. The truck steadied itself, then finally came to a stop only inches from a concrete wall.

I slumped over the wheel, physically and mentally spent, gulping air. I'd just caught my breath when I felt a hand on my arm.

Victoria looked me in the eye, her expression telling me everything I needed to know. She helped me out of the truck and led me over to Mac, Pip, and Pamela.

"This gang who you're hanging out with, Pop?"

I smiled and introduced them to her, then glanced around to see the two men were bound with their backs to the concrete wall of the enclosure. "What about Mendoza?"

"Gone. I would have liked to have brought him in, but this'll have to do," Victoria said.

"What do you mean, brought him in?"

"I'm sorry I couldn't tell you before. I've been working undercover for the DEA."

"I'm sorry, Vic."

"Sorry for what? You saved me." She ran her hand over my shirt, knocking some of the glass fragments from the windshield off. She turned her attention to Mac. "Anyone call this in?"

"I'm sure someone here saw it, which means it's time for us to go. Tru's probably drinking up a tab at the resort that I'm going to have to cover."

"You have my thanks, and if there is anything I can ever do to help you—" Victoria started.

"There's a long list, honey. Some you know and others you don't," I said. "There's Troy, then Kara, Kate and Tony, then Chase and—"

"You still have the boat?" she asked. "Maybe we could go sailing. Take some time, you know?"

"I think I'm done with boats after this last week." I reached out and hugged her.

EPILOGUE

SHAMELESS
STEVEN BECKER

I HANDED Troy the five hundred-dollar bills he had won at Dreamgirls.

"That's yours, Harvey. Fair and square."

"Let me know when it runs out."

Troy looked around at the group filing onto the Shark Key deck. "Oh, gotcha." He took the cash. "Seems like these seen some action." He fingered the worn bills.

"They have." That cash had traveled from Key West to Palm Beach and back to Shark Key in less than a week.

He grinned and placed the bills in the register behind the bar. "Step right up, y'all. Drinks are on Harvey."

"You didn't have to do this, Dad," Victoria said.

"It's the least I can do. Each one of these guys and gals helped me get you back."

Victoria and I hung back and waited until Troy had served everyone, then ordered a pair of Sam Adams. We settled with our backs to the bar. I leaned in toward her, giving a brief introduction to the characters scattered around the patio. The party was my thank you to those who had helped me.

The past week, even yesterday, already seemed like months ago. My injuries were still present, dulled some by the whiskey that Troy had plied me with before the others had arrived. Victoria was my focus, though I couldn't neglect my new friends.

Pip and Kara vied for the loudest person on the point. Their verbal sparring overshadowed the hushed conversation between Troy and Trufante, though I would be more interested in what that pair had to say to each other. They could easily be brothers from another mother—or even the same one, as things went in the Bayou. I could tell they felt the kindred spirit, too.

I watched as Troy Bodean stared across the flats, sipping his beer. I hadn't known him long, but I had figured out quickly that he wasn't a man to stay put for very long. He was antsy, ready to get back out there on the open road—or the open water, as it were.

I would miss the boat, but truth be told, that had always been Martha's thing. Besides, I had my little girl back and that was all that really mattered. Running into Troy had been the best thing that could've happened to me. Serendipity indeed. Taking me in and helping me save my Victoria was heroic, but he didn't care anything about that. He was just a decent human being. I looked around the bar, fighting back emotion. They were a bunch of decent human beings for sure, and I would never be able to repay them for what they had done for me.

Just then, Troy stood up, swallowed the last of his beer, and stretched his back. "Reckon I'll be headin' on out," he said.

"You're only having one beer?" Trufante asked. "At least put some in your cooler."

Troy shrugged and said with a wink, "It's already full."

Trufante shook Troy's hand and said, "I hope you find what you're lookin' for down in old Cayo Hueso, my friend."

And with that, Troy Bodean stood up and looked my way. With a tip of his hat, he walked down the steps to the west dock.

"Wouldn't ya know it," I said to Victoria. "The cowboy rode off into the sunset."

. . .

ON THE OTHER side of the room, Mac and Kurt were having a conversation with Kate, Tony, and Chase. I led Victoria over to properly introduce them all.

When I finished telling her how each had helped, I added a bit about those who hadn't been able to make the trip on short notice.

"We could have waited," Victoria said. "I would have liked to thank Isabella."

"I don't know that we'll see El Tigre again," Chase said. "I understand she's gone underground."

"Did Scar kill her?" I asked.

"No, I think he and his boss made her an offer. I don't know the details, because I don't want to. If you get my drift."

I nodded. "Kate, how are you?"

"My pride was more wounded than I was. Tony's made sure I rested up, and Whiskey hasn't left my side." She reached down and scratched the big German shepherd between the ears. "Thanks for coming to us. I wish we'd been able to stay and see this thing through, but it looks like you were in good hands all around. It's nice to meet the folks who made that happen for you, Harvey."

I shook my head. The gathering had been my idea. This saga needed to end, and this was the best way to put it behind us, as well as thank those who had jumped to our aid. "Best to get on things."

Victoria smiled. "That sounds like something my dad would say. So New England."

"I guess that's what I am."

"Are you going back?" Kate asked.

I hadn't had or taken the time to think about the future. One thing was for sure, though, there would be no boats involved.

"You know, I think that's where I belong." I paused, then turned to Victoria and asked the question that had been on my mind since we had been reunited. "What about you, honey?"

"If you're okay, I might go back with you. Maybe enroll in a graduate program in criminal studies."

I smiled at her. Having her come back with me was beyond my

wildest dreams. "You can get a Ph.D. just hanging around with the folks in this room."

She laughed and grabbed my arm. "You might be right about that."

Check out the next two books coming soon from some of your favorite

Tropical Authors

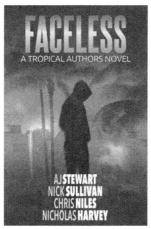

\

Made in the USA
Las Vegas, NV
01 March 2023

68323366R10105